SLOWLY THE RIVER FLOWS

HUANG ZHENG

Translated by
WU JIAMEI

Sinoist Books

Published by
Sinoist Books (an imprint of ACA Publishing Ltd)
University House
11-13 Lower Grosvenor Place,
London SW1W 0EX, UK
Tel: +44 20 3289 3885
E-mail: info@alaincharlesasia.com
Web: www.alaincharlesasia.com

Beijing Office
Tel: +86(0)10 8472 1250

Author: Huang Zheng
Translator: Wu Jiamei

Published by ACA Publishing Ltd in association with the Liaoning Children's Publishing House

Original Chinese Text © 江水静静流 *(Jiāng Shuǐ Jìng Jìng Liú)* 2017, Liaoning Children's Publishing House, Shenyang, China

English Translation © 2019, ACA Publishing Ltd, London, UK

ALL RIGHTS RESERVED. NO PART OF THIS PUBLICATION MAY BE REPRODUCED IN MATERIAL FORM, BY ANY MEANS, WHETHER GRAPHIC, ELECTRONIC, MECHANICAL OR OTHER, INCLUDING PHOTOCOPYING OR INFORMATION STORAGE, IN WHOLE OR IN PART, AND MAY NOT BE USED TO PREPARE OTHER PUBLICATIONS WITHOUT WRITTEN PERMISSION FROM THE PUBLISHER.

This novel is entirely a work of fiction. The names, characters and incidents portrayed in it are the work of the author's imagination. Any resemblance to actual persons, living or dead, events or localities is entirely coincidental.

Paperback ISBN: 978-1-910760-81-9
eBook ISBN: 978-1-910760-82-6

A catalogue record for *Slowly the River Flows* is available from the National Bibliographic Service of the British Library.

1
MUM'S LIAOLUO

Alone, I walked along the riverbank. In the early morning mist, the beautiful scenery loomed. Gently and softly, the sound of a fairy singing a *shan'ge* floated in the air:

> *Le ah le luo,*
> *Let me sing a shan'ge across the river.*
> *Wake the sun up with a silvery laugh.*
> *Get up very early, oh diligent one.*
> *Full are the pig and sheep pens and the barn of grain.*

Then a soft kiss fell on my forehead.

It was not from a fairy but from my mum. It was she who woke me up with her beautiful *liaoluo* song, and it was my mum alone who could improvise and change *Liao luo yee luo* in the first line to *Le ah le luo* in which *le* means 'son' in the Zhuang language; therefore, *Le ah le luo* means 'Son, my son'. My mum was waking me up affectionately with her beautiful voice. When she lowered her head to kiss me, her unbraided hair fell down on my face. I opened my eyes.

Seeing me wake up, Mum stood up and pushed back her hair, ready to go to the kitchen.

"I'm not awake yet, Mum." I closed my eyes again.

Mum couldn't conceal a snort of laughter and said: "How did a person who is not awake speak just now?"

"I'm indeed not awake yet!"

"Well, well, Mum will wake you up one more time!"

Whispering in my ear, Mum sang *Le ah le luo* again. How sweet and soft my mum's song was! I listened to it quietly with my eyes closed. Mum was a well-known singer in the county, and her *shan'ge* was the gentlest and sweetest of all. She kissed me again. I opened my eyes at once, stretched out my arms, clasped them around her neck and kissed her face. Under the flickering kerosene lamp, I saw my mum smile happily.

As I put on my clothes, I said: "Mum, I love to listen to your *liaoluo*, but I don't like Dad's *jiate*. It sounds like an old bull mooing."

Jiate was the *shan'ge* in our community. In the Zhuang language, *jia* means *shan'ge*, and *te* means 'male', so *jiate* in Mandarin means '*shan'ge* of men'.

"Who is talking behind my back? Do you think I'm still sleeping and you can talk about me like this?" From the neighbouring room came the masculine voice of Dad, but it was joyous anyway. He was not really mad at me, honestly.

I stuck my tongue out. I didn't know that Dad was already up, but I knew he must be listening to Mum's sweet *shan'ge* as well. I said: "Dad, Mum's *liaoluo* does sound better than yours. I've decided that when I grow up, I'll learn to sing songs from Mum – never will I learn from your moo-like *jiate*."

"Silly boy!" said Mum as she helped me with my collar. "Dad sings in the man's way while I sing in the woman's way. You're going to be a man when you grow up, a young man, so you're sure to learn from your dad."

"Does that mean I have to cry like a bull?" I asked Mum.

"Of course!" Dad replied loudly from the next room. "There are two bulls in our family – an old bull and a calf."

I hurriedly ran into the kitchen and saw the bowl of porridge that Mum had prepared for me. Then, I ran out of the door towards the fig tree in the darkness and picked a tender fig leaf. The fire in the kitchen stove was still burning cheerfully, and the porridge in the pot was simmering. I put the leaf a little closer to the fire, letting it slowly soften. I was going to use it as the lid for my lunch box – an enamel mug, in fact. I discovered that there were still quite a lot of pickles on the rice in my mug, so I put more than half of them into my parents' bowls.

Sitting nearby, Mum was combing her hair. When she saw what I had done, she said: "Save more for yourself! Don't you boys share dishes at school?"

"I've counted them – there are enough for everyone," I replied.

I covered the mug with the leaf, tied it tightly around the handle with a string and then drank my porridge. Mum had already twined her hair into a long braid and was ready to coil it on her head.

"Mum, let your braid hang down. You look more beautiful that way," I said. It was true – my mum was known as a beautiful daughter-in-law in our village. All of the aunts and uncles in the village said she was perfect, with her crescent eyebrows, big eyes, high nose and cherry-like, small mouth; the perfect combination and the slightest change would spoil her beauty. All of the women in the village admired her fair skin with a rosy glow, her black and shiny hair, and her pearl-like teeth. She was addressed as 'Beauty Queen of *Shan'ge*'. I thought my mum would be prettier with a long braid to her waist, but I never saw her do that.

Hearing my words, Mum smiled and said: "In the village, only girls wear a long braid. Silly boy, you're a young man now, and your mum is not a girl any more. I must do up my hair in a bun. Is that wrong? Doesn't it look good?"

As she said that, she piled her braid high on top of her head, into the shape of a big pine cone, which was the reason why people called this hairstyle a hair cone. I thought she looked neat and tidy – beautiful too. I stopped talking about it and continued with my porridge.

Once I became a fifth-year student, Mum had to get up before daybreak every morning to prepare my school stuff – to be precise, my breakfast and lunch. The elementary school in our village was too small with only one teacher. No matter how affectionate he was and how much he loved us, he could only teach us to the fourth year, so after we finished that year, we had to climb over a big mountain and walk ten *li* to Tuanlong Elementary School to continue our education. Ten *li* of mountain road! It was impossible for us to have lunch at home, so our parents had to prepare food for us very early in the morning. Dad had offered to do this for me, but Mum declined. She said Dad was working hard every day and needed more rest than her; besides, she was in charge of the housework. What's more, she said that while Dad was good at doing big things, he was not as careful as her with small things like cooking; he could never handle food just right. What if I had to make do with half-baked rice? How could I concentrate on my studies without any distractions?

I didn't want to bother my parents to do this for me and place an extra burden on them. I wanted to do it myself. But why couldn't I open my eyes in the morning? I didn't know the reason. Every morning, I couldn't wake up until I heard Mum's *liaoluo* in my ear.

Mum said: "Is there any child who doesn't like to stay in bed?"

It was in the early 1980s, and no household in the village ever had enough food to live on. To have an uneventful year, you had to be very economical with your grain. Even if you were economical, your stored grain at home might still be insufficient; if you were not economical, you were sure to suffer from starvation. If you didn't have enough food and you wanted to buy some, there was no way you would find anything at the market.

In the mornings, Mum could only cook like this: she used an iron wok with four helper handles to cook the porridge, which would be enough for breakfast and lunch for three people. She would still put the same amount of rice into the wok, but when the water was boiling and the rice was fully cooked, she would immediately take some rice out, put it into my mug and press it tight. When the rice cooled down and stuck together, it filled the mug to the brim. In this way, the porridge in the wok was sure to be much thinner. Mum often put some sweet potatoes into the porridge after I left for school. I hated to eat rice at school while my mum and dad would have to drink thin sweet potato gruel at home.

Mum said: "Lejiang, you're a student, and you need to fill your stomach."

Dad said: "We can manage it, but your study is worth more than gold."

Every day, except Sundays, Mum would get up early to prepare lunch for me – rain or shine.

As I was drinking my gruel, Mum said: "Lejiang, you boys get up so early every day and have to climb over Genma Ridge. Are you feeling tired?"

"No," I replied, though in fact we did feel a bit tired; after all, we were climbing up the side of Leimao Mountain. In the Zhuang language, *gen* means 'above' and *ma* means 'shoulder', so *genma* means 'on the shoulder'.

Mum added more firewood into the stove, and it crackled happily, putting a red light on her peaceful face. She stared at the fire and said softly: "Leimao Mountain is the highest peak in this area. The best one. Do you still remember – a young man of Zhuang turned into Leimao Mountain?"

It reminded me of the story my mum had told me before.

2

MAHUAI, THE GOOD YOUNG MAN

It was said that the place we were living in used to be a broad expanse of flat, fertile farmland and thick forests with singing birds and fragrant flowers – the most beautiful home in the world. The most remarkable thing was that a spring welled up from the earth in the green bamboo forests. Clean water flowed endlessly from it, providing not only something sweet for people to drink but also irrigation for about ten thousand *mu* of farmland. Grain barns were full, cattle and sheep packed the enclosure, and all the villages in the Zhuang community were enveloped in the joyous singing of *liaoluo*.

One year, the Queen Mother of the West wanted to brew the most aromatic and mellow liquor for her birthday party. She called the Dragon King of the South Sea, who was in charge of water and rain, to her palace and sent him to the human world for the cleanest and sweetest spring water for her liquor. The Dragon King dare not show slackness in carrying out her order, and he sent all his shrimp soldiers and crab generals to look for the best spring water in the human world. They searched and searched, and finally they found our spring. Without a word, they snatched the spring and took it to heaven.

Without water, the people and animals in the village would die of thirst, and the seedlings in the field would shrivel and turn yellow.

The Dragon King said: "Don't worry. It's nothing serious. I will create rain for you as compensation." As he said this, a downpour began.

The Queen Mother of the West was very satisfied when she got the spring water. She rewarded the Dragon King of the South Sea with a huge jar of liquor. The Dragon King was overwhelmed with joy when he saw this, and he drank it, one bowl after another. He kept on drinking and drinking until he became drunk and completely forgot about stopping the rain. The downpour continued for seven days and nights.

The Dragon King was sound asleep as the heavy flood attacked the human world. Seedlings were washed away, and so was the soil. After the flood, farmlands were nothing but fields of stones. When the Dragon King sobered up and took a look, he found two years' worth of rain had fallen. "All right," he said: "I will not send rain in the coming two years!"

As a result, the human world suffered again. A serious drought came after the flood. The ground was scorched, with flying sand and rolling pebbles everywhere. Even the birds were wailing *kow kow kow*.

People had a very hard life indeed.

There was a good young man named Mahuai, whose shoulders were as strong as a bull's and who was determined to save his village from suffering.

Mahuai started his journey. He walked and walked; he waded eighty-one rivers, climbed over eighty-one mountains, wore out the soles of thirty-six leather shoes, walked for forty-nine days and at last he reached the fairy mountain. He wanted to learn from the immortal how to save his village.

The immortal asked him what he wanted. Mahuai said his greatest hope was to regain the soil and spring water so that people could live and work in peace again.

The immortal said: "Well, let me teach you how to be a good bearer. But first I need to ask you: how much do you want to bear? Do you want a light load or a heavy load? And do you want to do it fast or slow?"

"The heavier, the better, and the faster, the better. Everyone in my village is suffering now."

"The heavier and the faster you choose, the sooner you will grow old and die. Young man, you have to think about this carefully."

"If I could bring back the soil and spring water for my village, I would rather die immediately," said Mahuai, firmly.

After learning from the immortal for three days and three nights, Mahuai could walk faster than a gust of wind and his strength was mightier than the sum of one hundred thousand bulls. The immortal gave him a pair of huge baskets and an iron pole before he left for his village.

Mahuai left the fairy mountain in a hurry. He didn't take a minute's rest and sped to the South Sea, where the soil of his village had been washed. When he got there, he loaded the soil into the baskets. His strength was astonishing – one load was two mountains on either end of his iron pole. With one load done, he grew three years older. He quickly carried the soil back to his village, emptied the baskets of soil onto the ground and then hurried back to the South Sea, without stopping.

Mahuai wanted to bring back all of the soil to his village as soon as possible and then flatten it with his pole.

When there were only two loads left in the South Sea, Mahuai discovered that his beard had turned white. He was worried that he wouldn't be able to come back again, so he uttered a great roar, summoned all of his strength and carried the two loads on his pole.

The moment he got to his village, the iron pole broke with a crack and became Duandan Mountain, which we saw every day. Mahuai didn't have time to flatten the soil on the ground, so we had mountains of similar size in this place.

Mahuai himself also fell down, and he became the highest mountain in our community.

The immortal was moved by the spirit and will of Mahuai. He put a hat on Mahuai's head to protect him from rain and sunshine.

To allow everyone to live a good life, Mahuai, the good young man, became our Grandpa Leimao Ridge. He didn't have time to shoulder the spring back, but when he carried the soil, he sweated quite a lot, and this became the Bachi River in our community. The water in the flowing river was the sweat of Mahuai, the good young man of our community.

Every time I thought of the story of Leimao Ridge, the scene of towering Mahuai, who shouldered the soil of our village and flew across the land, would appear in front of my eyes.

After she saw me finish my porridge, Mum tied my mug to my backpack and then handed it to me. She said: "To bring back the soil of our village, Mahuai sacrificed his life, running back and forth. Similarly, you boys go back and forth to school to master cultural and scientific knowledge so that you can build our village when you grow up."

"Mum, I get it!"

I hurried to the door. Today, I wanted to be the first one.

"Torch!" Dad shouted behind me.

I hurried back and took the torch from my dad.

3

A FOX, NOT A TIGER

I ran to the edge of the village and turned on the torch. Immediately, the bright light drew a big circle in the dark sky. I shouted: "It's time to go to school! Let's go!"

Instantly, a few voices responded to me from different directions: "Let's go to school!"

Thick clouds hung over the sky, so the moon and stars could not be seen. Everything was deeply buried in the darkness, including the Bachi River and surrounding mountains, high and low. Roosters crowed every now and again. Occasionally, dogs barked, sounding lazy and sleepy.

Wei Tianmin – we all called him Lemin – was the second to arrive. He hurried towards me, panting heavily. Reluctant to accept second place, he said: "Brother Jiang, you're so fast. I should have been the first one to be here. I was just half a step behind. What a pity."

Brother Jiang was me. My name is Huang Mingjiang, and because I was the eldest, all my friends called me Brother Jiang.

Qin Hanping was the third one to get there. We liked to call him Leping. He stuttered a little. The moment he arrived, he announced: "Everybody, I found a big secret, and now I'm going to tell you. Are you ready?" He stopped to keep us guessing and then continued: "Did you know that Third

Aunt's big rooster clucks when it crows. Just like this: *cock-a-doodle-doo, cluck*."

Lemin and I burst into laughter when we heard this. We didn't say whether or not we knew about it; we just followed Leping and crowed like a rooster: *Cock-a-doodle-doo, cluck! Cock-a-doodle-doo, cluck!*

Yisong, namely, Li Yisong, was the last one to arrive. He said: "My black dog is to blame. It insisted on coming with me. I drove it back, but it just wouldn't go away. It wasted too much of my time, so I'm the last one today."

Pretending to be serious, I teased him: "That's easy. When market day comes, ask your dad to sell your black dog. I don't think it would dare to drag you back next time."

"No way!" Yisong shouted eagerly. "He is my good friend. How could I bear to lose him?"

We all admired Yisong for having such a lovely black dog. It was a very smart puppy that could learn everything you taught him, and it understood how you felt. It was indeed adorable.

Everybody was present! We started off for school.

According to what we had agreed, the first one to arrive would walk ahead, leading the group, and the last one followed behind the others. The one who walked in front was brave and bold because he was leading the procession while those who walked in the middle felt at ease because they were escorted by friends fore and aft. But the heart of the one at the back often jumped with fear because he always felt he was being followed by a shadow, steps rustling – it was so scary. It did feel like this when you walked in the darkness. I knew Yisong was timid, so I said to him: "Yisong, let's swap places today. You walk in front, and I'll bring up the rear."

Yisong, however, was feeling quite brave. He said: "No! Let's follow the rule! I'm not a coward!"

Our village was named Najie. In our Zhuang language, *na* means 'field', and *jie* means 'ferns'. It is said that during the years when our village was under construction, our ancestors opened up a field that grew ferns. They named that field Najie, which later became the name of the village. Our village was surrounded by mountains.

To get to the nearest market in Baodong County, we had to walk twenty *li* of mountain road; by the waterway, it was more than thirty *li*. The route to our school was a winding, mountain footpath. In fact, no matter which direction you wanted to head from our village, a winding footpath was your only choice. One section of this pathway had a scary name: Tiger Trail.

In the 1930s and 1940s, tigers were still seen in our community. This section of the pathway was the only way for tigers to enter our village. The seniors told us that one day a tiger sneaked into the village at night and dragged a big pig away. There had been much discussion about how to deal with this tiger, but it disappeared silently and didn't come back. It was as if it had heard the people talking about it. When villagers talked less about the incident, the tiger stealthily entered the village on a dark, windy night and dragged another big pig away.

The whole village was shocked. What a tiger it was, whose intrusion didn't even stir up a dog to bark. From its footprints, the villagers found that the tiger had entered the village via the Tiger Trail – twice! So they decided to set a trap on the trail to catch it alive.

The trap was located two *li* away from the village, where there was a large bamboo bush. More than a dozen young men nearly broke their necks to bend the biggest and firmest bamboo stem down. They trimmed its leaves, tied a cord around it with a thick hemp rope, and then buried the cord in a pit they had dug on the trail. They set the trap and covered it with soil and some fallen leaves. Everything was restored to its original appearance. If you were not told it was there, you would never see it. All of the villagers – old and young, male and female – were informed about the location and power of the trap, and the notification went to the neighbouring villages as well. People near and far all knew that there was a trap near the bamboo bush on the Tiger Trail. The trap was set at night and disarmed during the day. Everyone had to be very cautious when walking at night. All except the tiger knew the trap was there.

But the tiger was really smart, as if it had become one of us human beings. One morning, the people were surprised to find that its footprints stopped about twenty feet in front of the trap and then turned right to avoid it. That was to say, the tiger had come at night, but it had seen through the plan and walked off without being fooled.

We all admired the tiger's smartness, but we continued to set traps. Young men improved the trap to make it less noticeable. They didn't believe the tiger would be so smart that it would get away again.

But the tiger did escape, and a man fell into the trap. That man was my grandfather's grandfather – my great-great-grandfather. On that day, he went to visit relatives in Tuanlong. They had a big banquet and drank and talked until very late. My great-great-grandfather insisted on going back home that night, saying he needed to work in the field early the next morning. No matter how hard his relatives tried to make him stay for the night, he said no. They finally had no choice but to tell him: "Tigers frequent the Tiger Trail. It's very dangerous. It's better for you to go back at dawn."

My great-great-grandfather was young, vigorous and impetuous, and he was a bit drunk at that time. When he heard them talking about a tiger, he looked up and argued carelessly: "Tiger? What's there to be afraid of? Isn't it a little bigger than a cat? Just a big cat! Who cares? So what!"

Seeing that he was drunk but could still maintain his consciousness, his relatives had to relent and let him go back to the village alone at night.

In fact, my great-great-grandfather was one of the young men who had set the trap, so he knew it was there on the trail, and so did his relatives. But it had been quite a long time, and they all believed it had been removed. Never did they expect that the villagers would be so tenacious and set the trap every night after so many years.

It was no wonder my great-great-grandfather fell into a trap that he had laid himself.

He walked all the way and muttered: "Tiger? Just a big cat! Where's the tiger? It's just a bluff used to scare cowards!"

Suddenly, something bit his leg.

"Damn it! The tiger did come!"

It wasn't the tiger but the trap. My great-great-grandfather had stepped on it. With a popping sound, the trap was triggered, and the hemp rope cord caught his calf without any mercy. The bamboo sprang up and suspended him in the sky, upside down.

"Help!" Great-great-grandfather broke out in a cold sweat and sobered up immediately.

Long and thick, the bamboo attached to the cord was so elastic that it flew up and bent down, and then flew up and bent down again. My great-great-grandfather was launched into the air and then bounced back to the ground. He was completely awake and knew he had become a 'two-legged tiger', caught by the trap laid by himself. He stopped yelling for help. Instead, when he was close to the ground, he tried his best to grab the grass on the roadside, hoping to stabilise his body but in vain. The bamboo stem had an amazing elasticity, and it repeatedly bounced back while my great-great-grandfather uprooted the grass he held tightly in his hand.

Many people in the village heard the faint sound of someone calling for help, but they didn't know what had happened and didn't go out to check. At dawn, they searched and found my great-great-grandfather caught in the trap. The bamboo stem had stopped bouncing upward, and my grandfather had stopped struggling. He was hanging upside down a few feet above the ground. All the grass near where he was hanging had been pulled out. It was indeed a hilarious scene. Everyone tried to suppress their laughter and hurried to put him down in a bundle.

My great-great-grandfather was the first one to laugh. He said: "That's funny. I became the tiger. A two-legged tiger. But you must be clear about one thing – I didn't steal any pigs."

Everyone burst into laughter when they heard this. It was said that some of the villagers laughed until their sides ached and some laughed until they cried. When they stopped laughing, they went to check the Tiger Trail. My goodness, the tiger had come back that night; the footprints started from the side of the river, followed great-great-grandfather all the way and stopped at a place not very far from the trap. It seemed it had crouched there for quite a while before it left. It must have witnessed the funny scene of my great-great-grandfather hanging upside down, and it must have smirked smugly when it finally left.

We walked over to the bamboo bush, shone the torch at it and saw several large bamboo plants gathered together, rising high into the sky. Amid the morning breeze, the bamboo plants huddled together, making rustling noises.

Lemin said: "Listen, it sounds like the cry of Brother Jiang's great-great-grandfather when he was hanging from the bamboo stem."

"It seems to be warning us of the tiger's footsteps," I added.

Yisong heard it and became panicked, his teeth chattering

"Brother Jiang, I, I…"

"Shall we exchange positions?" I asked.

"I… I… No." Yisong clenched his teeth and puffed out his chest.

When we were close to Genma Mountain, I pointed my torch towards the ridge in front of us and suddenly saw two green lights. We were taken aback and stood still.

Lemin had sharp eyes and uttered a low cry: "Tiger!"

"There, there is indeed a tiger," Leping stuttered. He was so frightened.

"Tigers don't bite people, do they?" Yisong was shuddering and tried to push his way behind us.

Four torches shone together on that pair of green lights. Luckily, it was not a tiger but a fox.

We four were relieved.

Yisong, however, dared not walk at the very end of the group again.

4
AN UNEXPECTED LETTER

It was still dark when we arrived at school. The entire campus was quiet, with nothing stirring. I hushed gently to everyone. Silently, we passed through the playground, arrived at the foot of the teaching building and then tiptoed to the second floor, where our classroom was located to the east. On the classroom door, the large black lock still hung there like a loyal soldier who was performing his duty. We swept the cement floor with our hands, blew off the dust and sat down in a circle in front of our classroom, cross-legged and heads together. In our school, there was only one class in our year, with a total of thirty-nine students before we joined. Now there were forty-three. We had made an agreement long before that we only turned on one torch, with the other three switched off in order to save batteries. Today, it was my turn to switch on the light. Holding my torch high in my right hand, I shone it downwards. We took out our Chinese books and began to read silently. We had arrived too early and were unwilling to wake up the sleeping campus or disturb our dear teachers who had been working hard for us all year round and might be sleeping right now.

An amiable voice burst out behind us as we were reading our books attentively: "You guys are here so early!" It was our principal, Mr Yang. He had begun the routine morning check. He also had a torch in his hand, but his had three batteries and shone brighter and farther than ours. We hurriedly greeted him and then fell silent, not knowing what to say next.

"Your classroom hasn't opened yet, has it?" Principal Yang asked.

I replied: "We are not on duty today. The student who is hasn't arrived."

Principal Yang smiled amiably and said: "Who else could be here so early except you boys!"

Leping blurted out: "You, Principal Yang!" What a silly boy Leping was! Principal Yang was not asking us a question but praising us! Leping didn't quite catch the principal's meaning.

"Well, I'll open the door for you. It's too cold to sit on the ground. Go and read your books in the classroom." Principal Yang held in his hand a bunch of keys that could open all the classrooms in our school. After he opened the door for us, he went to check the other places. We rushed into the classroom, put our school bags and lunch mugs on our desks and then sat together around one desk. It was still me who held the torch high, but this time we leaned over the desk in four directions rather than sitting cross-legged, and I read aloud in a low voice. We didn't have light bulbs in the classroom because in Tuanlong, like our Najie, there was no electricity at that time.

When we first transferred to Tuanlong Elementary School, we didn't go to school as early. We usually gathered together after daybreak and then set out from the village, but we would always be late for our first class. We all felt bad about this and decided to go faster on the road, but it didn't make much difference. No matter how hard we tried, we would still be late for class when we arrived at school, sweating heavily. Under the watchful eyes of our classmates, we announced our lateness at the classroom door and entered with our heads drooping. It was so embarrassing.

When Dad heard about this, he thought about it and said: "Let's set out earlier. To acquire real skills, you have to be the early bird."

Our parents had a discussion, and eventually they decided to help us by making early preparations so that we could set out before daybreak. Thus, we embarked on our ten-*li* journey every day before dawn.

At first, the adults worried about our safety, so they took turns to escort us. However, a few days later, we all voted against it. The twenty-*li* trip there and back was too much for the adults, especially when they still needed to work in the fields after they returned to the village. Wasn't it just a ten-*li* mountain road? Just high mountains and dense forests and rivers and fields to cross. There were no beasts that hurt people; we could walk to school on our own. Seeing our determination and knowing that we were already quite familiar with the road to school, the adults eventually agreed: "It's an opportunity for our kids to build their courage."

After that, we walked ten *li* in the dark every day except Sundays.

At noon, when our classmates scattered away to have lunch at home, we four would sit around a desk in the classroom, open our lunch mugs, and exchange dishes on the rice before we began eating.

One day, as we were doing this, Mr Ma, our teacher, entered the classroom, waving his hand towards us and saying: "There's a letter for you boys."

"A letter? Who would write us a letter?" Leping said. "Someone must have made a mistake."

I took the letter and saw on the envelope:

To: Huang Mingjiang, Qin Hanping, Wei Tianmin and Li Yisong, fifth year, Tuanlong Elementary School, Baodong Village, Yongning County, Guangxi Province.

From: Wei, Class 2, fifth year, Qili Village Yongning County, Guangxi Province.

I jumped up and said: "It's from Cuiyun." We put our lunches aside and hurriedly opened the letter. It read:

Gejiang, Geping, Geming and Yisong,

How are you? I feel I have left our home town for a long, long time. I miss all of you every day and miss the ten-*li* road to school we used to walk together. The school here is very large, with a huge playground; the classrooms are large too. We have a lot of teachers and students. Every night, I dream about you and our trip to school, singing along before dawn. The lunches you brought to school and shared with me were delicious! How are you getting on with your studies? Can you keep up with the other students? Are you all happy? Did the Bachi River rise?

Sincerely, Wei Cuiyun

Each of us held the letter and read it aloud once. After we finished reading, we remained silent. Then, each of us read it again in a low voice. Still no one said anything; we bowed our heads as we ate. Lunch on that day was flavourless, and we all felt lost.

5
CUIYUN, A GOOD CLASSMATE

Cuiyun was a few months older than Yisong. In fact, there was less than a year's difference between us, so we were all in year five. In the beginning, the five of us went to study in Tuanlong Elementary School, and Cuiyun was the only female student in our group. Cuiyun was even more timid than Yisong. On our way to school, we always let her walk in the middle in case she would feel frightened.

One morning before dawn, it drizzled and it was especially dark – so dark that you felt you could not breathe. We were only halfway down the road, on Genma Ridge, ready to climb down. I was at the end of the group, and Cuiyun was in front of me, the next to last one. She suddenly turned around and whispered to me: "Brother Jiang, I want to pee."

Lemin, who was walking in front of Cuiyun, heard it too. He said: "That's easy. Girls always need to go first. We boys can just move on – when we pass Genma Ridge, you can take your time doing it."

Cuiyun replied nervously: "No! No! Don't leave me alone. I'm scared."

I looked around and found there was a small rose myrtle bush nearby, not tall but good enough to hide behind if you squatted there. I said: "Cuiyun, go and pee behind the rose myrtle bush. We'll be here waiting for you."

Cuiyun immediately said: "No! There are thorny wild grasses there, and perhaps snakes too!"

Yisong said: "Sister Cui, what about peeing here? We'll stand around you in a circle to protect you."

Cuiyun refused. "No! That would be too embarrassing!"

Leping, who led the group, said: "What about coming to the very front? We'll move on after you've finished."

Anxiously, Cuiyun said: "How could I do that? The urine will stink!"

Leping said: "If you don't want to go to the front, you can only go and do it at the back."

That was the last choice for Cuiyun. She was very hesitant. She murmured: "The back…" But she could not continue because she was so nervous.

It was then that I saw a small piece of open space near the roadside. I stopped and said: "Cuiyun, there's an open space near the back of our group. What about coming here? I'll stay here with you, and you can grab my trouser leg so you won't feel scared."

Cuiyun said: "You boys mustn't look back!"

I replied: "Don't worry! We promise you." It was pitch-dark, so even if someone dared to look back, what could he see?

Lemin said: "We'll move on and Brother Jiang will stay here with you. Is that OK?" As he said this, he and the other boys walked forward. They didn't turn on their torches, and in a blink of an eye they disappeared into the darkness.

Cuiyun stepped into the open space and squatted in the darkness. I switched off my torch and then felt her hand trembling as it seized my trouser leg tightly. It was as if she was afraid every second that I might leave her alone. She must have been holding it in for a long time. She squatted beside me for quite a while and then stood up, saying: "I'm OK, Brother Jiang. Sorry for all the trouble!"

I said: "There's no need to feel embarrassed! All living people need to poo and pee. Otherwise, they would be dead."

"Hey! Brother Jiang, stop talking about dead people. I'm so scared!" cried Cuiyun in a low voice.

That was Cuiyun – such a lovely and timid girl.

Cuiyun was docile and quiet, but although she looked elegant and understated, she secretly worked very hard to compete with everyone. Her school performance was always above average. Of course, like us, it was a challenge for her to study at Tuanlong Elementary School, and it was a pity that she didn't have the chance to go on fighting with us.

Did she have another choice? Her family fell upon hard times. When she was very young, her father went to work in the mountain and suddenly became ill with a disease called intestinal colic. He died very quickly, leaving the whole family in a miserable condition, especially little Cuiyun. I didn't understand what kind of disease intestinal colic was and why it was so horrible. I asked my mum why I could survive it once after she had used a smooth-edged plate to scrape my body. I remembered that my skin was blemished and bruised, and then I recovered. Mum told me it was because no one in the mountain knew how to cure this disease and Cuiyun's father's type happened to be the most serious that would always kill people. Later, I knew there was a serious disease called cholera, and I think that's what Cuiyun's father had caught. He died very unexpectedly. A few years later, Cuiyun's mother remarried. Her new husband was from another village, and she wanted very much to bring Cuiyun with her to his family. But by then, Cuiyun had grown up and begun to learn things. She knew when a mother remarried, a child from her previous marriage would be called *tuoyouping*, 'a burden', and she was not willing to become that. She refused to go with her mother and stayed to live with her grandmother. Her grandmother loved her very much, but she was old and weak, and it was not easy for her to feed herself and her granddaughter, though life for them was not so hellish as to be unbearable. We all knew of their suffering. Gentle and quiet as Cuiyun was, she was extraordinarily tough. She loved to study and went to school every day, even if she had no textbooks, pens, pencils or exercise books; she just sat on the ground and listened to class with her head held high. She always put some of her saliva on her fingertips to practice writing characters on the ground. Our teacher particularly liked her; he bought her textbooks and arranged a seat for her. We liked her as well and shared our exercise books and stationery with her. In this way, she quietly finished years one to four in the village. Then, she went to study at Tuanlong School with us.

Cuiyun's grandmother couldn't afford to buy a torch for her, so we let her walk in the middle, using four torches to light the road for her and to protect her.

Neither did her grandmother have the money to buy her a school bag or material to make one. Cuiyun made a hemp rope and tied her books together to carry them to school and bring them back home each day. When my mum heard about this, she sewed a school bag for Cuiyun with some silk cloth she had woven herself; it was the same size and appearance as mine. In my mind, my mum's hand-made school bag was the best in this world, a priceless treasure. I cherished it. I remembered it was on that night when everyone came to my home to review homework and do school assignments. In Tuanlong School, all fifth-year students were required to attend evening class. We lived far from the school, and it was impossible for us to go back there, so all my friends decided to meet in my home and do our homework together. Our teacher, Mr Ma, appointed me as the captain of us five, partly because my house was spacious; my mum kept it clean and tidy, and the tables and stools my dad made were very comfortable. Everyone liked to come to my house. Of course, I was the eldest, a month and three days senior to Lemin, so they all called me Brother Jiang and enjoyed being with me and listening to me. My dad even bought us a bright bamboo-shoot lamp, that is, a large kerosene lamp with a high shade that looked like a bamboo shoot, hence its name. Even now, I can remember when Cuiyun came to my home one night and Mum handed the new school bag to her, saying: "Cuiyun, I made you a school bag. You know, I'm not good at it – I hope you like it and make do with it." I noticed Cuiyun's eyes immediately light up, but then tears fell down. She flung herself into my mum's arms, trembled all over and cried: "Aunt, Aunt..." My mum didn't say anything; she just patted her back gently, her eyes turning red.

Cuiyun's grandmother didn't have money to buy Cuiyun a lunch mug. Cuiyun cut down a bamboo tube and made herself one with her delicate hands. I never saw Cuiyun bring any rice for lunch; every day, she brought to school a bamboo tube of porridge – extremely thin porridge. And no dishes at all. Every day, when we four boys sat around eating together, Cuiyun just carried her bamboo tube and went to the hallway outside the classroom. There she sat, silently drinking her porridge alone without any of the exhilaration or joyous laughter we had when we shared dishes with each other. Seeing that, I felt upset, and so did my friends. We had a secret discussion, and eventually we worked out a plan.

The fourth class the next day was physical education. When the bell rang for the break, we four rushed into the classroom and shouted: "It's so hot! We're thirsty!"

As if discovering a new world, Yisong shouted: "Sister Cui has porridge!" With these words, he picked up Cuiyun's bamboo tube and poured the porridge into his mouth.

Cuiyun appeared at the classroom door. She was shocked and didn't know what to do. We had planned it and chosen the perfect time.

Yisong continued: "It really helps!" As he said this, he was about to have another swallow.

"Let me try!"

"Let me try!"

We ran to him, trying to have a share of Cuiyun's porridge.

When the bamboo tube was passed to me, which was actually part of our plan, I took a sip, pretended to look into the bamboo tube, then looked at Cuiyun, who stood still at the classroom door and said: "Oh, no! There's only half a mouthful of porridge left. Guys, what do you think we should do?"

"We have to compensate Sister Cuiyun for this."

"Yes, we should!"

"Yes, we must!"

I said: "Cuiyun, we are sorry. We were so thirsty that we forgot everything and drank up your porridge. What about having lunch with us today?"

Cuiyun smiled and walked over. She didn't get mad at us, and I knew she wouldn't. On the one hand, Cuiyun was good-tempered; on the other hand, we were all childhood playmates and classmates, and anyone who knew this would not get angry at all.

When I saw that our conspiracy had worked, I lifted the fig leaf, spread it on the desk and put a large lump of rice on it, saying: "I took the lion's share just now!"

Yisong continued: "I was the first to drink the porridge!" He put a large lump of rice on the leaf as well.

Lemin said: "I have a big mouth, and I'm the one who should give Cuiyun the most."

Leping added: "I was the one who felt the most thirsty."

Cuiyun grabbed Leping's hand and said: "No more rice for me! That's too much for me! I can't finish it."

I handed Cuiyun a pair of chopsticks, which I had prepared for her. I had long noticed that she never brought chopsticks. You know, she had porridge every day, and she had no dishes either.

Sitting around a desk, we five began to eat lunch together. We usually gobbled our food quickly, but when we saw Cuiyun eating slowly, chewing and swallowing carefully, we slowed down, assuming good manners, like gentlemen. Of course, this pretence would not last long, and we soon showed our true colours.

After Cuiyun finished her meal, she smiled, raised her head and said: "It was delicious!" I thought it must have been quite a long time since she had rice for lunch.

Yisong asked hurriedly: "Sister Cui, my lunch is delicious, isn't it?"

Cuiyun said: "Yes, it's delicious."

Lemin continued: "How about mine?"

"It's yummy too!"

Whoever asked her about the food, she gave a positive answer. I smiled secretly. She had a mixture of our food, so how could she tell the difference?

After that, we always had our lunch at school like this. We first drank the porridge Cuiyun brought to school, then we shared our rice with her. We five sat in the classroom, eating happily and heartily. After we finished, we four boys would make comments on the dishes whether they were delicious or not. Of course, none of us had the final say, and the conclusion was based on Cuiyun's words. Surprisingly, her verdict was always: "It's delicious!"

6
A RACE IN THE MOUNTAIN

We could hardly do without Cuiyun. It was she who had brought courage and peace to our group. When we saw her sitting in the classroom quietly, we felt her determination and perseverance, and we didn't have any excuse to shrink back. We knew that if she had hesitated or wavered a little, she would never have overcome so many difficulties and continued to study in the classroom with us.

We four boys were good classmates and childhood playmates. Of course, it was inevitable that we would sometimes quarrel or even fight with each other, but it was Cuiyun who helped resolve our disputes quickly.

One day, on our way back home from school, when we had just climbed over Genma Ridge and saw our beautiful village, the Bachi River appeared in front of our eyes, flowing slowly onwards around our village. Leping began boasting as he walked. "Yesterday, I saw a wild hare when I herded the cattle in the mountain. It turned back and ran away quickly, and I chased after it and almost caught it. Aren't I good? I tell you guys, no one can compete with me when it comes to running in the mountain."

The previous day was a Sunday, and I had helped with the housework at home. I didn't know whether Leping had really gone out to herd the cattle or not, and neither did I know whether he had chased after a wild hare. But I was clear about one thing: he was bragging, and I didn't fall for it at all. So I questioned: "Almost? What do you mean by almost? By two *li*?"

Yisong said: "My little Blacky once chased after a wild hare and caught it, but he is no match for me. Am I better than you?"

Lemin couldn't refrain from saying: "My dear classmates, please remember one thing – it's not good to brag in front of me."

Talking like this, we eventually stopped and had a heated argument, with no one willing to make concessions and no one succeeding in convincing the others.

Cuiyun was walking at the front. She turned back and asked: "Can't you boys just drop it and move on?"

Too busy to pay attention to her, we continue bickering.

Cuiyun laughed softly and said: "You boys should stop arguing. The Bachi River is going to flow backwards if you continue. Now, give me your school bags and lunch mugs!"

We stopped quarrelling and looked at each other, not knowing what she meant.

Cuiyun said: "It's no use arguing with each other. Why don't you have a race? I'll take care of your bags and lunch mugs. You boys set out at the same time, and whoever arrives at the immortal's head first is the winner."

The immortal's head that Cuiyun spoke of was a small mountain. In our community, mountains had interesting names. One group of mountains was named The Immortal Watching the Moon. Indeed, viewed from Genma Ridge, these mountains resembled an immortal, with a head, shoulders, a chest, an abdomen and two legs stretching into the river, lying on its back along the riverside looking at the moon. Roads passed through the immortal's belly like a fluttering belt. What was even more interesting was that there was a large pit on the upper section of the road and dense trees grew inside it; this looked like the navel of the immortal when viewed from afar.

I thought our ancestors were so clever to name the mountain The Immortal Watching the Moon.

We placed our school bags and lunch mugs beside Cuiyun, and, with our sleeves rolled up, waited for Cuiyun's order: "Three, two, one, go!" And off we went. This place used to be a pasture for herding cattle; there were no tall trees, but it did have some small bushes. We left the trails and began to run on the grassy slope. We rushed down the mountain, crossed over a stream and jumped over some field ridges. When we arrived at the belly of the immortal, we passed the navel and ran upwards. It was steep, and my legs felt so heavy that I couldn't even lift them up. My legs wouldn't listen to my commands. The expression 'run like the wind' did not apply in this case, and it was even an exaggeration to say that I was running – I was actually just walking. No matter how many attempts I made, I was unable to make big strides. It was as if I were marching on the spot. I looked around and found my friends were doing no better than me. When we arrived at the top of the immortal's head, we were all sweating and panting like dogs. Sprawling on the ground, we became four 'urchins watching the moon'.

We didn't recover until Cuiyun arrived at a leisurely pace. When we had calmed down and our heartbeats had returned to normal, each of us sat up, forced a smile and looked at Cuiyun, waiting for this graceful referee to announce the result.

"This is Brother Jiang's bag; this is Brother Min's…"

Cuiyun returned the school bags and lunch mugs to us first and then said: "I have seen clearly. You guys were almost the same, though Brother Ping was a little faster, and Brother Jiang was a little slower. But the routes you took were different. Some routes had long grass, some had short grass, and some had dense trees, while others were less dense. So I think you have all earned first place."

"We all came first!" we cheered, as we jumped together.

"But Yisong, in my opinion, did the best job!" added Cuiyun.

We all looked at Yisong, who was overjoyed but pretended to be embarrassed and said: "I often run on the mountain with Blacky, so I'm more comfortable with the mountain road."

We all agreed. There was indeed a difference between running on the mountain and walking on the road. We were convinced.

I said: "Yisong, you deserve the first prize."

"Yisong won first place!" we cheered, as we ran back home together.

Within a few days, our opinions were divided again. This time, it was about swimming. It happened like this. We watched a film, and there was a documentary before the main presentation, which was about a swimming competition. We learned that there were different styles of swimming, like breaststroke, butterfly, freestyle and backstroke. The problem was, what kind of style had we used when we were swimming in the river? After making comparisons again and again, I thought it was a kind of breaststroke.

Everyone agreed, but after a while, Yisong shouted: "Wait! Breaststroke means your two hands stroke backwards at the same time while ours do not – our two hands stroke backwards in turns."

We thought about it and felt he had a point.

Lemin said: "Shall we name it 'pig style'? I've seen pigs swim like that, with all four feet splashing around in the water."

Leping said: "Don't dogs do it the same way? We could call it 'doggy paddle'."

Yisong said: "I've even seen mice cross the river in a style quite similar to ours. Let's call it 'mouse style'."

It reminded me of the Sundays when we crossed the river by catching the tail of a bull. I said: "Bulls do it in a similar way. Bulls are the biggest. Let's call it 'bull style'."

What everyone said made sense, and each stuck to his opinion, making no concessions.

Cuiyun said: "What's the difference between those names? You all can swim, and any name is fine. But I can't swim, and if I happen to fall in the water, I'll sink to the bottom like an iron weight."

We were all surprised to hear that. "You don't know how to swim?"

Cuiyun said: "Did I have someone to teach me how to swim?"

Yes, who could have taught Cuiyun? It was my dad who taught me how to swim in the Bachi River.

7
THE BEAUTIFUL BACHI RIVER

All of the children in our village – boys and girls – had to learn how to swim, and they could swim across the Bachi River with their bare hands. It was a tradition passed down from generation to generation, and there were good reasons for it. Our village was located beside the Bachi River. As we were living close to it all year round, it was better to be safe than sorry. If you could swim and knew the waters, you would be able to save your own life when you got into difficulties in the river.

I could swim before I went to school, and the Bachi River was the swimming pool in which I learned and practised.

I always wondered why the river was named Bachi. Was it because it was eight feet wide? How could that be true when it was more than twenty-four feet wide! I once asked my dad, but he didn't know either. He said: "It probably means 'very small', doesn't it?" I was not convinced. In my mind, the Bachi River was the longest river in the world. No matter where you went, you would not find any river that was longer than our Bachi River. Of course, I changed my mind after I went to school. I discovered that we had the Yellow River and the Yangtze River rolling to the east, and they were both much longer and wider than the Bachi River. Later, I went to the Yangtze estuary, which was as wide as the endless sea. I thought the person who had named the Bachi River must have seen the Yangtze River first and been to the Yangtze estuary. Anyway, Bachi, the name of the river, read smoothly no matter how we said it. I liked it, and so did all the others in our village.

Dad told me the Bachi River flowed from a mountain called One Hundred Thousand. I asked him why the mountain had that name. Were there really one hundred thousand mountains like Leimao Mountain? In my mind, since there was a good reason for Leimao Mountain to have its name, there must be some logic behind the name One Hundred Thousand.

Dad replied vaguely: "Well, when we say thousands of people go to the fair in Baodong during the New Year Festival, we don't count the number exactly, do we?"

Anyway, there were a lot of mountains; if there were not one hundred thousand to be exact, there would be at least ninety-nine thousand and nine hundred! Having thought about it, even if there was only one spring flowing from one mountain, there were at least ninety-nine thousand and nine hundred streams! No wonder the Bachi River had been flowing for thousands of years so inexhaustibly. I was sure it would continue to flow and flow for thousands of years more.

From One Hundred Thousand Mountain, how many roads and how many turns had the Bachi River taken before it passed our village? I often stared at the silent, flowing river, pondering things like this. Sometimes, when the river was swollen with floodwater, I would sneak up to the river's edge, sit on a big stone, and watch the floating tree roots swirling up and down in the turbid water, thinking about which ones had been washed down from One Hundred Thousand Mountain.

In fact, there was more than one name for the Bachi River. In a place one hundred *li* from our village, it was called Fengting River, which meant a colourful phoenix flew there from One Hundred Thousand Mountain. Of course, people living beside the Fengting River wanted it to settle down there, but it wouldn't, though it did feel attached to that place. It flew on and on, and when it reached a place about forty or fifty *li* away from us, it had a new name: Sangjiangkou. This was where the Fengting River and the Zhulong River merged and became a wider and larger river: the Bachi River. At first, it was more like a little sister who loved to cry and throw a tantrum, but when it reached our village, it became a gentle and beautiful elder sister. She smiled and flowed silently past our village, and when she flew over the rocky shoals, she would hum softly with dimples on her face.

On both sides of the Bachi River were thick woods and clusters of bamboo plants that surrounded the water like two beautiful, green, silk belts. Farmland beside the river exhibited different colours – sometimes green, sometimes yellow and sometimes white, like a beautiful landscape painting that changed constantly. That was the Bachi River I loved most.

I learned to swim in the river totally by chance.

On that day, I was on the way to the threshing floor with my father and mother. As I walked on, I suddenly thought of the dream I had had the night before. I said: "Dad, I had a strange but interesting dream last night."

Dad was curious and asked: "An interesting dream? What was it about? Could you tell me?"

"Dad, I'm about to tell you. Well, it was like this. In my dream, I carried a large bag of food – rice wrapped inside a banana leaf. Mum prepared it for me. I was not to herd the cattle but to go to One Hundred Thousand Mountain. I went to the mountain by myself and searched everywhere for the source of the Bachi River, and I found it. Then I rode on a huge log and drifted down from its source. I drifted and drifted, faster and faster, and suddenly a huge wave threw me up, high into the sky, so high that I could even touch the smiling faces of the stars. Then I fell down onto a pile of straw with a loud flopping sound. I opened my eyes, and it turned out I had fallen into my mum's arms."

Mum and Dad both laughed when they heard this.

Mum said: "It feels better to be in Mum's embrace, doesn't it? Even in his dreams, my Lejiang falls into Mum's arms!"

Dad asked: "You rode on a log?"

"Yes, a huge one with two branches on its top, like the two horns of an ox. I held the branches all the way, and it was very steady."

Dad continued: "Why didn't you swim down the river?"

I was speechless. After a while, I said with embarrassment: "Dad, I don't know how to swim."

Dad and Mum looked at each other and said together: "It's time for Lejiang to learn how to swim."

As soon as I arrived at the threshing floor, I forgot everything. My friends and I chased after each other, and some of us rolled over on the stacks of rice straw. We just played until we itched all over our bodies, while the adults, of course, were engaged in threshing, working like devils. Strangely, although all of them sweated heavily and their clothes were wet as if they had been soaked in water, they still had the strength to sing *shan'ge*. Men shouted *jiate* like oxen, and once they had finished, the women continued with *liaoluo* softly. After that, they all laughed out loud, continued with the songs and then laughed again, on and on.

"Dad, you're working so hard, don't you feel more tired when you sing and laugh loudly?" I asked.

Dad said: "Lejiang, you're too young to understand this. When you grow up, you'll do the same."

I really didn't understand because I hadn't grown up yet. I dropped the subject and played with my friends again. Of course, my friends were Lemin, Leping and Yisong. Sometimes, Cuiyun would join in, but she usually left quietly after playing with us for a short while. She had to go back home to help her grandmother with housework and a lot of other things. The uncles and aunts all said that Cuiyun was a good girl, that there was no other child who could be more diligent than her, and that she would definitely be a good daughter-in-law when she grew up. I had no idea what a daughter-in-law was – I only knew they were all my good friends.

The other kids, like Brother Sheng, Brother Liang and Brother Chuan, were all older than us, and they were middle school students. They said we were little monkeys who knew nothing, and they would not play with us. To be honest, we weren't interested in playing with them either. There were also some kids who were younger than us, and they were indeed little monkeys.

The adults worked on the threshing floor until five o'clock in the afternoon. I didn't have a watch, but I knew it was five o'clock because I heard the tinkling bells that announced the end of the day at the elementary school in the village.

The men all went to take a bath in the river, leaving the women to clean the threshing floor.

"Mum, that's not fair!" I said.

Mum smiled and said: "Silly Lejiang, it is fair. When your father and uncles finish washing themselves, they will go back home to cook, and your aunts and I will go and take a bath to our hearts' content, for as long as we want. As we don't need to cook the dinner, we might even swim across the river."

My mum was not bragging. She and her friends could all swim, and they were not inferior to the men. This was a characteristic of our village and, in fact, of all the villages along the Bachi River.

At that moment, a pair of large hands reached for my armpits, and, with a loud "Hey", I was held up high by my dad and then placed to sit on his shoulders. Then I found Lemin, Leping and Yisong were all sitting very proudly on their fathers' shoulders.

In a short while, we arrived at the Wangpa Ferry to cross to the other side of the river and get to our village. When the Bachi River reached there, it took a sharp turn and created a very deep pool. *Wang* means 'deep pool', so the name Wangpa literally means 'a deep pool called *pa*'.

The riverbank on that side, close to the ferry, was gravel because the sand and mud had been washed away by the water. It was more than a metre deep right near the shore. On the other side of the river, a lot of fine sand, washed from upstream, was deposited, and it formed a gentle slope. Everyone liked to swim near the ferry because there was no sand at the bottom of the water, and no matter how many people jumped into the water to swim, the river remained clear. The people of my village were good swimmers, and they were not afraid of deep water at all.

When we arrived at the river's edge, all the adults jumped in, while we children knelt beside the river, scooping water with our hands to see who could splash the furthest.

My dad and his friends stood in a row in the water after they had washed away their sweat. They said to us: "We're going to sit in the water. Pay attention and watch us!"

With these words, they sat down in the river. The water covered their shoulders, then reached their ears, then their heads. Very soon, they sank under the water and disappeared.

We all stared at the river, our eyes popping out. The river was as still as a mirror, and occasionally a few small, silvery-white fish jumped out of the water, drawing small circles one after another on the surface.

It had been quite a while since they disappeared under the water, and we could not see them anywhere. We were so nervous that we dared not make a sound – we just stared at the river, which seemed to be quieter than usual.

We waited and waited. It had been a long time, but still there was not any sign of them.

Yisong burst out crying first: "Dad! Dad!"

We became more panicked. Our fathers had disappeared! They had been swallowed by the Bachi River! We shouted together: "Dad! Dad!"

The other uncles, who were sitting beside the river, seemed more alarmed and began to talk about it. "Oh, no! Where could they be? Have they all disappeared?"

Then, in the middle of the river, our fathers poked their heads out of the water! I could see they had secretly dived and then swum a long way. We didn't know how long they had been gone, but it seemed longer than a day – so long that we were scared by it. They stood in the middle of the river, shouting together: "We're here!"

Then they swam back so fast that they were with us again in the blink of an eye.

We broke into laughter and threw ourselves into our fathers' arms, regardless of the consequences. In other words, we all jumped into the river!

Dad caught me and held me up. He asked: "Lejiang, tell me, is swimming fun?"

"Yes, it's fun."

"Let's learn how to swim so you won't need to ride on a log in your dream. You could swim down the river yourself, directly from One Hundred Thousand Mountain! What do you think? Do you want to learn?"

Without a second thought, I replied: "Yes!"

"Good! Let's do it now."

As he said this, he held me and walked into the deep water until it reached his chest. He then turned around, placed me on the surface of the water and held my chest and belly with his hands. He said: "I'll hold you, so there's nothing for you to be afraid of. Stroke the water bravely!"

Imitating what I had seen the adults do, I stroked the water hard with my hands and kicked my legs vigorously. In order to avoid choking, I struggled to raise my neck to keep my nose out of the water. One stroke after another, it felt so wonderful. In a very short time, I had swum back to the shore!

I stood on the shore and shouted happily: "I can swim! I can swim!"

All my friends were learning hard with their fathers' help too. The river echoed with our excited shouts.

Dad smiled and said: "Great job! Shall we do it again?"

"Yes, please."

Like the last time, Dad held me and let me swim back to the shore. He said: "Don't puff out your cheeks. Open your mouth to breathe, then you won't choke so easily. Don't raise your head so high – otherwise, you'll get tired. How do you feel this time? One more try?"

I was in high spirits; how could I stop trying? So we went back to the starting place and tried again. This time, I didn't raise my neck or close my mouth, and I felt more relaxed. But it felt like I was swimming slower and slower.

When I swam back to the shore, I panted and said: "Dad, I tried as hard as I did last time, so why did I get slower?"

Dad laughed loudly and said: "Lejiang, it was me who brought you back to the shore those first two times. This time I didn't. Sure, you were slower than before, but you swam back by yourself. That is pretty good!"

"Dad, let's do it one more time, shall we?"

"Of course, let's go."

As I swam, the shore was close to me. Suddenly, my dad pulled back his hands from under my chest. I struggled to carry on, but my legs were out of control and seemed to be dragged down under the bottomless water. I was in a panic and blurted out: "Dad!"

I heard Dad say: "Lejiang, don't panic! Swim towards the shore, hard!"

Was I swimming? The truth was that I was struggling, up and down in the water. The river choked my nose and my throat. I coughed and shouted: "Dad, help!"

Dad didn't reach out his hand but said: "You're almost there! Swim hard! Harder!"

I struggled and swallowed a few mouthfuls of water. Then, I stepped on something: the solid river bed near the shore. I hurriedly staggered up, and when I reached the shore, I squatted down, my nose running, my eyes sore and my head buzzing. I coughed loudly, once, twice, trying hard to get the water off my chest. I felt so bad!

Dad said: "Take a rest!"

He then left me alone and swam back to the river. When he poked his head out of the water, he began to sing his *jiate* again.

Liao luo wei,
Eagles can't have strong wings unless they practise flying;
Tiger cubs can't run dextrously unless they practise running;
Children will never grasp the skills to secure a promising
    future unless they undergo intense training.

His singing still sounded rough and a little hoarse, quite like the moo of an old bull.

I recovered while my dad swam back to the shore. I felt I had almost drowned. To be completely honest, I felt I had actually died in the river.

Dad asked: "Are you feeling better now? How was it? Do you still want to swim?"

I wiped my face and rubbed my eyes silently. To be honest, I was a bit scared, unwilling to drink the water in the river like this.

Dad stood in the water and looked at me, saying "Lejiang, just now, you swam about a *li*, all by yourself! That's awesome! You did it by yourself – you're great! Practise a few more times, and I'm sure you'll be a good swimmer."

"The river... the river is too deep!"

"That's why we should learn to swim! No matter how deep it is, we can swim across it, can't we? I think you're scared, aren't you?"

I looked at him and nodded with embarrassment. I admit I was really scared.

Dad said: "You'll get choked by the water before you can swim well, and it's a lie to say it's not scary, but, Lejiang, you should keep one thing in your mind – the more frightened you are when you're facing difficulties, the more you'll be bullied by them and you'll fail to accomplish a single thing. You were choked by the water, and you're scared, so you might not swim for the rest of your life. It works for everything. We can't admit defeat in the face of difficulties. If we don't, we're sure to win eventually."

Seeing me saying nothing, Dad continued: "When I held you, you could swim quite well. In fact, you could still swim without my help. Remember the third time? Didn't you swim by yourself when I barely touched you? Why couldn't you swim well when you realised I had taken my hands away from you? It's because you were in a panic and you had lost confidence in yourself. Just think about it. Am I right?"

I turned it over in my mind and realised my dad was right. When I saw him take his hands away from me, I was afraid and panicked, and my legs voluntarily went down, trying to step on the solid ground…

I looked up and said: "Dad, let's do it again."

"I won't hold you this time!"

"That's exactly what I want! I want to swim by myself."

Dad was very happy. He said: "Good! You have guts! That's my boy, indeed!"

Dad held me in his arms and walked towards the river for about two or three metres. He then said: "I'm going to let you go. Open your mouth to breathe. Calm down and swim!"

I cut through the water forcefully and made up my mind not to let my legs slip down.

Splashing around in the river and choked by a few mouthfuls of water, I coughed violently, but I managed to swim to the shore. I gasped and felt so tired as if I had used up all my strength, but I was very happy because I could now swim by myself!

I wanted to do it again. Suddenly, the sweet sound of the *liaoluo* of my mum and her friends could be heard in the distance. My friends shouted together: "It's time to go home!" They were already sitting firmly on their fathers' shoulders.

Dad said: "Mum is coming. It's time to shift. Let's go back home to cook dinner. You've got your whole life ahead of you, and as long as you stick to it, there's nothing that you can't learn."

On our way home, I asked my dad how he learned to swim when he was a little boy. Dad laughed and said: "Well, it's very simple! It was in the same place where you learned to swim just now. My father – your grandfather – pointed at the river and said to me: 'Have you seen it? This is the river, and you need to make sure you know where the middle is and where the bank is. Swim back by yourself. Crawl if need be, or you'll be eaten by the fish.' As he finished his words, he picked me up and threw me into the river."

Sitting on my dad's shoulders, I stuck my tongue out when I heard that. "Did Grandpa really throw you into the river?"

"Yes, he did," Dad laughed. "I fell into the river like a stone and immediately choked. I'd be lying if I told you I was not panicking at that time. I hurriedly paddled with my hands and struggled to poke my head out of the water to see where the riverbank was and where my dad was. I just paddled and paddled, and it seemed like a year had passed. I don't know how much water I swallowed, but I eventually got back to the shore."

I truly admired my dad. He was so awesome! After that day, I went to practise swimming with him a few times, and I got better and better. Then, I wanted to experience being thrown into the river, and I asked my dad to do it to see if I could manage to swim back to the shore. Dad seemed a little hesitant. He smiled and said: "Well, I don't have the same strength as your grandfather had. I can't throw you that far. It's better for you to swim out and swim back yourself." My dad had powerful arms. I knew he just didn't have the heart to throw me into the river.

The adults asked us to swim in the river with our clothes on, saying sometimes we might fall into the river like that. It was not too difficult for me. You just felt a bit heavier and a little awkward with wet clothes on, but it wasn't too difficult.

8
A SMALL BAMBOO RAFT

The task now before us was to teach Cuiyun to swim. It was still hot, the best season for swimming. If we didn't seize the chance, the weather would turn cold as autumn and winter came, and it would be impossible to swim in the water. We decided to hurry up.

But where could we teach Cuiyun to swim?

Of course, Wangpa Ferry was the best place, but it was very deep there, and we four were not as tall and strong as the adults, so we knew we could not protect Cuiyun in the deep water. Our parents had warned us that we should never do anything dangerous.

After talking it over, we finally agreed to teach Cuiyun to swim in the fish pond.

In our village, there were two kinds of fish ponds. One was called *wu*, a very deep pond that had water all year round and contained a lot of big fish. The other was called *tun*; these were shallow – the deepest part would only reach your chest, and the water would dry up every spring. After people had finished catching fish and shrimps, they would use a *tun* to cultivate seedlings until they grew strong and green. Therefore, the bottom of a *tun* was quite flat, and it was very safe for swimming. Rest assured, the adults loved to see us playing in a *tun*.

We finally chose a fish pond named Tunmeizhang. In the Zhuang language, *mei* means 'tree', and Tunmeizhang is literally 'camphor tree fish pond'. Cuiyun was happy to learn to swim in this fish pond because it was located on the way back home, very close to our village. It was perfect for us too: we could teach Cuiyun how to swim, and, at the same time, we could have a bath in the pond. Because it was on our way back, we had enough time to stop to swim and then run home to help with housework, which was especially important for Cuiyun. Compared with us, she had much more work to do for her grandmother.

"We'd better not bother that beehive near Tunmeizhang," said Yisong with a shrug.

Near Tunmeizhang, there was an old longan tree, at the foot of which was a hole where a beehive was located. Looking through the cup-sized entrance to the hole, we could always find some glittering honey inside which was so tempting that it always made our mouths water. I once ventured to reach my hand into the hole, trying to get some honey out to taste, but the bees were so angry, and I was stung badly that time. Most of my friends had similar experiences, and we were all afraid of doing it again. As for the adults, their hands were so large that they could not fit into the hole, and they didn't want to hurt the longan tree. As a result, the beehive was there, safe and sound, and it grew bigger and stronger.

"As long as we leave it alone, we won't get into trouble!" I said. "Let's wade in immediately! Let's get started today!"

We ran to the fish pond, quickly took off our clothes, except for our shorts, jumped into the water with a splash and swam away.

I turned back and saw Cuiyun still standing beside the pond, having no idea what she should do.

I stood up in the water and shouted to her: "Cuiyun, get into the water! Be brave!"

Yisong shouted: "Sister Cui, come in and join us. It's very comfortable in the water. The pond is very shallow, and you won't drown."

Cuiyun was still hesitating. I swam back to her side and said: "Take off your clothes and get into the water. Don't be afraid. We'll protect you."

Cuiyun blushed and said: "I don't want to take off my clothes." As she said this, she went into the water cautiously. I thought it was understandable: Cuiyun was a girl, and she would of course feel embarrassed to wear only shorts like us in the water. I said to her: "It's all right to swim with your pants on, but what if your blouse gets wet – you don't have an extra one here, do you? What about taking off your blouse? You can't learn to swim very well with your blouse on either."

Cuiyun agreed. She turned around, quickly took off her blouse, placed it on the shore and walked into the pond with her hands covering her chest. She was in such a hurry that her whole body was soon immersed in the water, with only her head above the surface. I stole a glance at her and found there was no difference between Cuiyun's body and ours. I really didn't understand why she was so embarrassed.

Cuiyun began to learn to swim. Two of us stood on each side of her, trying to hold her body and move slowly forward as the adults did for us when they taught us how to swim. Like us, Cuiyun closed her mouth tight, puffed her cheeks and flung her arms and legs in the water. She was choked by the water, and she coughed until her eyes turned red. Unlike us, she didn't say a word; she just nodded her head when we spoke to her. She only shook her head when we asked her to take a rest.

We practised in the fish pond every day after school and then went back home to help with housework. Although we didn't have a lot of time to practise, Cuiyun learned wholeheartedly and earnestly. It was another example of the tenacity that she had developed since she was very young. She also found there was no difference between her upper body and ours after she took off her blouse, but every time she went into the water, she would still protect her chest with her hands and immerse herself in the water in the blink of an eye.

It didn't take long for Cuiyun to swim a little skilfully. She no longer puffed her cheeks nervously; instead, she opened her mouth slightly and breathed steadily. She would even look at us and smile secretly when she was in a happy mood. She often took part in our competitions as well. Of course, she always came in last, but she didn't feel sad and said it would be embarrassing if she won over her teachers.

Being called teachers, we proudly stuck our noses high in the air.

One afternoon, our teachers had a workshop, and we were dismissed from school earlier than usual. Walking on the mountain road, I suggested bringing Cuiyun to swim in the Bachi River since we had enough time. Everyone agreed with applause. Cuiyun said she was a little scared, but she could not resist the temptation of the clear Bachi River, and she went with us happily.

We arrived at the Wangpa Ferry, but I dared not let everyone swim there because it was so deep, and I didn't think it was safe without adults. We needed to swim on the other side of the river where the water was shallow and the bottom was flat and smooth with fine sands.

We untied a bamboo raft at the ferry and asked Cuiyun to sit on it, holding our clothes in her arms while we held the raft, two on either side, paddling together to push it to the other side of the river. We just watched a film called *Sparkling Red Star* and had learned the song from it. At first, it was Cuiyun who was humming the song softly, and then we four joined the chorus. We couldn't sing the song in tune; we were just shouting:

> *Small bamboo raft floats on the river,*
> *Passing high mountains on both sides.*
> *The red stars are shining brightly,*
> *Guiding me to the front to fight.*

The sky was blue, and so was the water. A few egrets croaked to each other. They flew through the green trees by the river and stopped to rest on the high bamboo tops, going up and down like a few naughty children sitting on a see-saw. As we pushed the raft forward, it moved slowly, the water rippling alongside it. The sun shone across Cuiyun's face, making her look like a gorgeous flower. This was such an impressive sight that it became deeply engraved in our hearts, leaving us a memory that would never be forgotten.

We spent an unforgettable afternoon, playing to our hearts' content, having a water fight in the crystal clear water.

Cuiyun didn't participate in our game; instead, she just practised swimming back and forth silently, over and again, never getting tired of it. Later, she stood in the river, brushed back her wet hair, scooped a handful of water from the river and drank it with a sweet smile. Then, she said: "Our Bachi River is so beautiful!"

When we all had enough fun and were tired, we began to push the raft back to the other side of the river. As usual, two of us on either side pushed the raft while Cuiyun sat on top of it, wearing a look of excitement and happiness. She looked straight in front of her and combed her wet hair with her hands. The water dripped from her hair and dampened her collar, chest, shoulders and back, and quite a few places on her blouse, as if the Bachi River had embroidered her clothes.

Yisong said: "Sister Cui, I've never seen you swim so well! Indeed, you swim better than me now!"

Hearing that, Cuiyun replied with embarrassment: "How could I swim better than my teacher? But today I had a feeling that swimming in the river is completely different from swimming in the fish pond. I don't know why, but it seems more natural to swim in the river."

Leping said: "Of course it's different. That's why it's called the Bachi River and not the Bachi Fish Pond."

Could this be a reason? We all laughed when we heard it. Leping laughed too and scratched his head, embarrassed. When he did this, the raft lost its balance and slanted in his direction.

"Hey, watch out, Leping! Stop mucking around!" shouted Lemin, who was on the same side as me.

Leping made a few quick paddles to bring the raft back in balance.

I said: "Let's swim in the river whenever we have time in the future, shall we?"

Lemin said: "Great idea! The adults wanted us to learn to swim when we were young so that we could be like fish in the river."

I said: "We need to follow the adults' instruction and never swim alone in deep water or rapids. Let's swim in the shallows in future, shall we?"

Cuiyun said: "Without your company, I dare not do it myself anyway."

The moment the raft reached the shore, I saw Dad, Uncle Bomin, Uncle Boping and Uncle Bosong running to us quickly.

Dad said: "You're all here? Great! Come with us and catch some big fish, will you?"

At this time, we noticed that Dad was carrying a net on his shoulder, and so was Uncle Bomin and Uncle Boping. Uncle Bosong held in his hand a long wooden pole, on top of which was tied a lump of water pepper. I knew water pepper, which tasted spicy, was often used to drive fish out of their hiding places because they didn't like its smell.

Seeing the water pepper, we knew they were going to catch big fish, and we were all excited.

Cuiyun, however, declined. She said: "I can't go with you. I have to go back home to help my grandma with the housework."

Dad said: "All right, Cuiyun, you go back first. It's very considerate of you to think like this at such a young age!"

I said: "Cuiyun, would you please carry our bags back to the village in case we get them wet?"

Carrying all our bags and lunch mugs, Cuiyun went back. As she walked on, the four lunch mugs collided with each other, tinkling all the way.

Suddenly, I remembered something and shouted towards Cuiyun in the distance: "Cuiyun, you must come to eat fish in my home tonight!"

"To my home, Sister Cui!" shouted Yisong.

"To my home!" Leping had the loudest voice.

"To my home!" It was Lemin's voice.

"OK!" Cuiyun replied. Within a minute, her back was lost in the green trees.

"Ha ha ha," Dad laughed. "Our young men have invited a guest to eat fish, but the big fish are still swimming in the river! How generous you boys are!"

"What if we should fail to catch the big fish?" asked Uncle Bomin.

"Then we will have to kill a chicken to entertain our guest!" said Uncle Bosong.

I blushed and said: "Dad, surely you and my uncles are not so incapable."

"What?" shouted Dad. "You're trying to get even with me, aren't you?"

9

WHAT A HUGE FISH!

With the four adults, we set out on two separate boats towards Laili Sandbank, which was located downstream from Wangpa Ferry. My dad and Uncle Boping were the captains of the two boats.

Laili was a long and narrow rocky sandbar about ten feet wide. The stone had a flat and smooth surface, and the river flowed across it quietly. The water either side of the stone was at the same level, and the river ran without any change; therefore, if you weren't paying attention, you might fail to notice that there was a rocky sandbar there. When it hadn't rained and the river hadn't risen, you could easily wade, via the stone, to the other side of the river. When the dry season came, foxes could run through the shallow puddle on the stone to the other side of the river as well. In our language, *lai* means 'sandbar' and *laili* means 'a sandbar that foxes can run through'.

It was here that my great-great-grandfather – our ancestor who had hung for a whole night when he was caught in the tiger trap – had once single-handedly repaired a watermill, from which he could make an extra income by grinding grains for the villagers in his spare time. The watermill had long been abandoned, and the wooden planks used to stop the water had long disappeared, but the deep troughs carved to fix the planks were still on the stone, and so were some wooden frames that were used to pile stones in the river. A solid stone mill on the riverbank, two millstones and the round stone trough to grind grains had stood there tenaciously, refusing to disappear with the passage of time.

My dad had an idea: he wanted to rebuild the old watermill on the Bachi River and make it operational in this new era. But he didn't want to do it himself. He went to talk with Uncle Bomin, Uncle Boping and Uncle Bosong and told them he thought that we children were working very hard in school and it was quite possible that we would further our education at a higher-level school. We were still at the stage of compulsory education when parents did not need to spend much money; but after this stage, it would cost more and more, and the burden on each family would become heavier and heavier. Our country and society would provide some financial support for poor rural students, but we couldn't always rely on this. My dad suggested everyone work together to build a watermill and save all the money earned by grinding grain to support all the children in the village to go to school. The four of them reached an agreement immediately and decided to start in the coming winter holiday. They wanted us to participate in the construction of the watermill in order to let us face up to the test of life and learn to work hard to build our own future. They had already made a plan: when the winter holiday came, the first thing was to prepare all the wooden boards for building the dam. The four families would need four large saws – one each for an adult and a child to saw the pine board. Today, they would go to Laili to do the measuring work in order to make a more detailed plan.

When my great-great-grandfather built the watermill, he found there was a fairly deep and large cave with a narrow opening behind the rocky sandbar in the river. Almost every year, one or two sesame catfish could be found hidden inside the cave. Sesame catfish was a unique species of fish there; it had no scales, black spots on its body and jagged bony thorns on its dorsal and pectoral fins. This kind of fish was very sluggish and couldn't swim fast. It liked to ambush, waiting in the cave for its prey and then making a sudden attack. The underwater cave in Laili was the ideal place for them to stay. They could grow extremely large, and they lazily hid in one spot all day long. I heard that my grandfather's father had once caught one that weighed forty-seven *catties* and nine *taels*, a record that has never been broken! This custom had been passed down from generation to generation, and we weren't sure how many sesame catfish had been caught from this cave.

After our fathers had thoroughly checked all of the details and taken everything into consideration, they went swimming in the river. My dad took the opportunity to dive into the water, and he found the cave. He felt the entrance and immediately concluded that there was a sesame catfish inside. They quickly moved a stone to block the entrance. Locked in the cave, the big fish couldn't escape.

We sailed the boat to Laili and pulled it up near the rocky sandbar. Dad dived into the river again to check the location of the cave. Soon, he came out and said: "It's there."

I hurriedly took off my clothes and said: "Dad, let me have a look."

"Sure, it's time for you to learn how to locate a place."

Following my dad, I dived in. When the light passed through the water, it became darker, but I managed to find the cave. The entrance was the size of a small bucket – too narrow for a man to get in – and it was blocked by the stone. I felt it with my hand and didn't find anything unusual.

When I rose above the water, my dad asked: "Could you feel there's a fish in the hole when you touched the stone?"

I shook my head. I didn't feel it.

"Experience is accumulated every day!" said Dad. Then, he called my friends over and instructed: "All of you go down and take a look. You boys need to work together to catch big fish in the future."

Lemin and the other boys followed my dad, dived into the water and then quickly came back up.

Yisong said: "It's so deep – I couldn't even find the entrance to the cave."

My dad said: "The cave is located in the deep water where sesame catfish will feel safe enough to hide. If it was in a shallow place, even small fish would not like it. Do you remember where the cave is?"

We looked around to make sure where we were and then nodded.

"Then stand by and watch how we catch fish!"

Dad waved to Uncle Bosong, who immediately jumped into the water holding the pole with a water pepper. They leaned side by side, hands gripping the stone with only their heads rising above the water. Uncle Bomin and Uncle Boping cast three nets above Dad's and Uncle Bosong's heads, one after the other. Then, Uncle Bomin and Uncle Boping dived into the water to check whether the nets had covered the entrance of the cave and were secure enough that the fish couldn't escape.

I asked: "Dad, why did you cast three nets?"

"Our nets are made from twine, and one of them would not be strong enough because the fish could tear it apart and break away. If that happens, what are you going to serve to your guest?"

"Dad, please can we go down and check the nets."

With the nets above his head, Dad said: "OK, but it's very deep – don't force yourself to dive to the bottom if you can't make it. Uncle Bomin and Uncle Bosong are checking the nets right now, so you boys can wait here."

We dived into the water again and groped along the nets to check them. The water was indeed quite deep, and we couldn't hold our breath long enough, so we had to rise to the surface quickly.

At this time, Uncle Bomin and Uncle Boping came up after they had finished checking the nets from two different directions. Wiping water from his face, Uncle Bomin said: "All three nets have covered the entrance tightly – there are no loopholes."

Uncle Boping added: "I've checked it inch by inch, and everything is all right."

Standing on each side of the nets in the shallow water, Uncle Bomin and Uncle Boping grabbed their edges, getting ready for the fish. Dad dived into the river, and immediately we heard the sound of the stones colliding under the water. We knew my dad was moving the stone away from the cave entrance.

Very soon, my dad poked his head out of the water, inside the net. He said to Uncle Bosong: "The stone has been moved away from the hole. It's your turn now. Remember, don't stand square to the entrance – otherwise, the fish will knock you down when it dashes out."

Hearing that, my heart pounded faster. I stared at the water nervously, wondering whether there would be a fish so big that it could knock an adult over? I took a look at my friends, and they were all shocked as well, with their mouths wide open.

After a while, Uncle Bosong appeared next to Dad. He said: "My pole has touched the fish and it feels very soft – probably its belly. I think it's a very big fellow, very powerful. It just won't come out."

Dad said: "Let me try!"

He took the wooden pole and dived into the river again. We became even more nervous.

It felt like ages until we saw my dad poke his head out of the water. He gasped for air and panted: "I felt it too. It seems it's not afraid of the water pepper – a strange fellow indeed!"

Before my dad had finished speaking, Uncle Bomin and Uncle Boping shouted at the same time: "Here it comes! What a huge one!"

The big fish rushed out of the cave unexpectedly and then knocked the top of the cast net fiercely. Its huge, flat head dashed out of the water into the net and then sank again. Dad and Uncle Bosong quickly dived into the river and pulled the edges of the three nets. The four of them worked hard together and hauled the sesame catfish onto the boat.

And what a colossal sesame catfish it was!

Our small boat sailed back along the river amid the sunset glow, and we sang the song *Returning from the Shooting Gallery* happily. As we sang, we made up our own lyrics.

> *The sunset reddened the clouds in the west.*
> *After fishing, we are sailing back to the village, to the village.*
> *The fish in the boat is long and big,*
> *Joyous singing flies in the air.*

Dad said: "Great singing! Now listen to ours!"

As he finished, he began to sing, and of course the other uncles sang along loudly with him.

> *Liao luo wei,*
> *The small boat dashes on the river,*
> *Bringing laughter back to the village.*
> *Why are we so happy?*
> *Because we have caught a big fish, as big as a fat pig.*

After we arrived home, we weighed the fish: it was forty-five *catties* and seven *taels*!

Mum said to me urgently: "Lejiang, go and invite your grandparents here to drink fish soup – otherwise, they'll be too full after they've had supper. Quick!"

Dad added: "Come back as soon as you've seen your grandparents! I have something for you to do!"

Nodding at their instructions, I ran out of our home.

My grandparents lived in a newly-built house belonging to my youngest uncle. The elders in our village liked to live with their youngest son. My youngest uncle was still a bachelor when my grandparents went to live with him. After that, he got married, and my grandparents began looking forward to grandchildren. However, my uncle and aunt-in-law went to work in Shenzhen – they were the first people in our village to move away for work. They wanted my grandparents to live with them in the city, but my grandparents declined; they decided to stay in the village and take care of their home for them.

When I came back home from my grandparents' place, Dad and the other uncles were still attending to the big fish. The first thing they did was distribute the fish to the elders in our village, which was a tradition. No matter who should catch a big fish, all the elders in the village would get a share. Now the fish cut for the elders was ready; it came from the rear half of the fish, each piece weighing more than one *catty*, thick and round like a small chopping board. Dad pierced a short bamboo strip through the cut fish and then twisted it at the end into a handle so that we could carry it to the elders. This task had to be assigned to us boys so that the tradition of our village would be imprinted deeply in our hearts and preserved forever. This was what my dad was referring to.

I walked over to my dad and said: "Dad, let's give two shares to Granny Cui, shall we? She doesn't have anyone to catch fish for her."

"Hey! You boys have been thinking the same thing! Don't worry – we have already taken it into consideration. Two shares for Granny Cui, one of which is for Cuiyun!"

I realised that while I had been to my grandparents' place, Lemin, Leping and Yisong had talked about this with the adults. In fact, even if we hadn't mentioned it, the adults had already planned everything.

Uncle Bomin, Uncle Boping and Uncle Bosong began to divide the fish for our four families. They cut the fish head and left it, together with the fish's insides, to my family because it was my dad who had found the fish and he deserved to be given more. Then, they divided the remaining fish meat into four portions, each family having a share.

Dad said: "Stay and eat sour plum fish head soup at our home tonight!"

Uncle Bomin, Uncle Boping and Uncle Bosong all declined because they had made their own arrangements.

"Well, then you have to listen to me!"

My dad put the fish head in front of him, lifted his knife and cut it into four parts in the blink of an eye. He placed the four parts, one by one, onto the four fish piles and said: "Everyone goes back to cook fish head soup! But I want to tell you that you will never make a better one than Meijiang does!"

Mum blushed when she heard this. She snorted and said: "Stop bragging! I'm miles behind Meimin, Meiping and Meisong!"

Dad continued: "All of the children like eating fish vesicles, guts and livers. Everyone takes some back." He then divided the fish insides into four parts as well. "Done! You boys are in charge of distributing the fish now!" Dad decided who was going to take the fish to whom. Following his instructions, we lifted the fish and ran out.

Dad stopped me. "Lejiang, wait a minute. Bring one more and send it to our neighbour, Uncle Bofu!"

Dad cut a large piece of fish meat, tied it on a bamboo strip and handed it to me.

10
IT'S HARD TO SAY GOODBYE

The porridge Cuiyun brought to school for lunch was always quite thin. Lemin told us that he could even count how many grains of rice were in it. Now it was getting thinner and thinner. We knew that life for her and her grandmother was getting harder.

I tried to cheer Cuiyun up. "Cuiyun, don't worry," I said. "We'll always be here for you. You must never give up. Come to school with us even if you don't have porridge for lunch. As long as we have food, you'll have a share."

Cuiyun nodded and said: "Brother Jiang, you're all so nice to me!" As she said this, her eyes turned red, and she tried her best to hold back her tears.

We told our parents about Cuiyun's situation and they all supported our decision. They said: "You five go to school together – you're brothers and sisters. No one is going to be left out!"

When they prepared lunch for us in the morning, they put as much rice as they could into our lunch mugs; while at school, we always tried to give Cuiyun as much food as we could.

The day when Cuiyun couldn't even bring porridge to school came quickly. Though she sat in the classroom quietly and listened attentively as usual, I could see panic in her helpless eyes. When we finished the fourth lesson, Cuiyun grabbed her bag and said to me in a hurry: "Brother Jiang, I… I want to go back first."

"No! We can't let you go alone. Even if you want to go, you should finish lunch first."

Yisong said: "Sister Cuiyun, let's eat first. Without you, our food is flavourless!"

Lemin and Leping had already divided their meals, and they said: "Let's eat! We're starving! Cuiyun, come on!"

Cuiyun lowered her head and shared the lunch with us.

Though we were all prepared for this, we ate with heavy hearts and there weren't the usual giggles and playful noises. We seemed to have become adults all of a sudden. For the first time, we knew hardship and the rocky road on the journey of life.

When we arrived at Genma Ridge, we took a short break, sitting on a big rock and wiping the sweat off our foreheads.

Ahead of us in the distance was our Najie Village and our winding Bachi River. Behind us was the school we had just left. It was five *li* each way – a total distance of ten *li* from our village to our school. We five were walking on this ten-*li* road in order to study, and we couldn't stop. We would go on our journey, step by step.

I said: "Cuiyun, let me tell you one thing. We're walking a long way to school, which, in a sense, is quite like swimming in the river. We're swimming forward, albeit very slowly and with great difficulty, and we'll make it as long as we don't stop. If we give up and don't move our arms and legs, we'll certainly not go any further, and we'll probably sink. You've been walking from first year to fourth year, step by step – please go on and finish the ten-*li* journey to the very end."

Keeping her head down, Cuiyun said: "I know, and I want to go to school, but it's so difficult for my grandma to do that for me."

Lemin said: "Don't be afraid. We'll help you."

Leping said: "Yes! You don't need to bring your lunch from now on. We'll share the lunch like today – it's enough for all of us."

Yisong said: "Sister Cui, we have no choice but to try to swim on, and we can't afford to sink!"

Cuiyun nodded with tears in her eyes.

From that day on, we set out to school from our village based on Cuiyun's schedule. We didn't start until Cuiyun came, no matter when she would appear. If she didn't show up, we would go to pick her up. For a few mornings, Cuiyun hesitated to go with us, but then she began to arrive as early as she did before. She didn't have a torch so she dared not come first, but whenever she heard someone shout, she would hurry over in the darkness. Our group still managed to arrive at school before dawn.

I remember one night about two weeks later, when everyone gathered in my home and did our school assignment together as usual. When we had finished our homework and were ready to go back home, Cuiyun burst into tears as she packed up her school bag. We looked at each other, not knowing what had happened.

Cuiyun wiped her tears and said: "Brother Jiang, Brother Min, Brother Ping and Yisong, today is the last day that I will study with all of you. I'm leaving tomorrow, and I can't bear to say goodbye to you all."

We were shocked. Looking at each other, we didn't know what to say.

After quite a while, Leping said: "Cuiyun, why are you leaving us? Are you afraid of walking in the darkness? Are you afraid of going to school?"

Yisong asked: "Sister Cui, is it because you don't have enough food for lunch?"

I didn't know what to say. I just looked at Cuiyun who was weeping miserably. As far as I knew, she seldom cried.

Cuiyun said: "I really don't want to leave you!"

This was what had happened. Cuiyun had an aunt – a cousin of her mother – who was a teacher in a primary school in another place. Knowing Cuiyun and her grandmother's situation made her heart ache, so she decided to bring them to live with her so that she could take care of Cuiyun's grandmother, and Cuiyun could receive an education. To avoid any fuss, her aunt did not let Cuiyun tell us until the day she was due to leave.

I felt glad for Cuiyun because from now on she had someone who could look after her, and she didn't need to worry about life any more; she could concentrate on her studies. But when I thought that we were going to be without our lovely younger sister on our way to school every day, I felt empty.

I said: "Cuiyun, no matter where you go, we all need to study hard and try our best to catch up with the other students. Don't fall behind!"

After my friends left, I couldn't hold back my tears any more. I tried desperately to control my feelings in order not to cry out. I didn't know why I was crying.

The next morning when we were about to set off, Yisong said: "Sister Cuiyun hasn't arrived yet!" For a moment, we all stopped, turned around and took a look towards the direction of Cuiyun's home, but we all knew that she would never again come to school with us on the ten-*li* mountain road.

11
A LION IS IN THE WAY

In her letter, Cuiyun asked: "Can you keep up with the other students?" There was a reason for her to ask this question. It was because we had all encountered difficulties with our studies after we transferred to Tuanlong School. These were not just small difficulties – they were huge! At that time, all of us, including Cuiyun, worried so much about this, and we didn't know what to do.

The ten-*li* mountain road was not a difficulty. We could defeat it. We walked along the road happily, and it became more familiar and shorter with each passing day. As we walked on, the long journey had turned into a short trip that we could easily accomplish by finding better pathways up the mountain. The departure time was not a difficulty. We could handle it. We were happy to set out earlier. After the embarrassing 'late report', we always finished our ten-*li* journey before dawn, and we never missed our first class. But when it came to difficulties with our studies, we were floundering.

Language was the first problem. We lived in a small, remote village in the mountains, and we spoke the Zhuang language. Though it has been mixed with quite a lot of Mandarin Chinese, it has very distinctive characteristics of its own. In grammar, there are some differences between the Zhuang language and Mandarin Chinese.

Let's take terms of address as an example because this is a very interesting aspect of our Zhuang language. When you're a child, people put *le* ('son') or *yi* ('small') before your name, while a group of children is called *le'nuo*. When you get married and have a family, you're addressed with the name of your first child. In my family, for example, my dad was called Bojiang (*bo* meaning 'father'), and my mum was called Meijiang ('mother of Jiang'). My grandfather was called Gongjiang (*gong* meaning 'grandfather'), while my grandmother was called Pojiang (*po* meaning 'grandmother'). It's the same when you have a daughter; after Cuiyun was born, her father changed his name to Bocui, and her mother was called Meicui. The rule is simple: place 'father' and 'mother' in front of the first child's name. This applies to brothers and sisters too. Cuiyun called me Brother Jiang, and she called Yisong Younger Brother Song, or simply Yisong. We called Cuiyun Sister Cui or by her name. I felt attached these terms of address, so I was reluctant to change. There are some special terms too; for example, my grandfather was called Gongda, my grandmother was Yadai, my paternal aunt was Ban'niang, and my paternal uncle was Nong'niang.

When we spoke Mandarin Chinese, we had to translate it first. For example, *qian'man* means 'in the sky', but in the Zhuang language, *qian* means 'go up' while *man* means 'sky'. Translated literally, *qian'man* becomes 'go to the sky' rather than 'in the sky'. The word 'pork' is another example. We use *nu'mu* to refer to pork, (*nu* meaning 'meat' and *mu* meaning 'pig'), but its literal translation is 'a pig raised for meat'. Here's another example: in the Zhuang language, 'sun' is *ta'en*, in which *ta* means 'eye' and *en* means 'sky', literally translating as 'eye sky'. In fact, it should be translated as 'the eye of the sky'. What a big difference!

Our classmates were basically Han Chinese, and they all spoke Pinghua, a trade language in some areas of Guangxi and also a second language of the Zhuang people. Pinghua and Mandarin Chinese are basically the same, with only slight differences in tone. When our classmates spoke and wrote, they would say or write whatever came into their heads without making any mistakes, fluently and smoothly, which we all admired so much. Things were different for us. We all thought in the Zhuang language, so before speaking and writing, we had to translate what we wanted to express into Mandarin Chinese. It was no wonder we fell behind our classmates. When answering questions, our classmates were eloquent and loquacious, while we four were still busy translating. We didn't dare raise our hands and offer to answer questions.

Another obstacle for us was intonation. We had spoken the Zhuang language, with its own particular intonation, since we were born. Without proper training, we all had a strong Zhuang accent when we spoke Mandarin Chinese.

Once, Teacher Ma gave us an assignment in his language class. We were required to write a short essay describing our campus, and we would have the chance to read our essays in class if we raised our hands fast enough.

During the evening class, I read my essay to my friends, and they all said it was pretty good.

Yisong said: "Brother Jiang, raise your hand tomorrow. We have never raised our hands before."

I agreed. We couldn't always fall behind the other students like this.

In class the next day, sitting at my desk, I was full of confidence. When Teacher Ma encouraged us to put up our hands, I raised my right hand immediately.

A forest of hands shot up in the classroom, and I thought that mine would be unnoticeable, but Teacher Ma spotted me. It was probably the first time he had seen one of us do that. He looked very happy.

He said: "Put your hands down. Now, let's invite Huang Mingjiang to read his essay."

I stood up, cleared my throat with a little dry cough in an attempt to calm down, and then read aloud the essay I had spent a long time preparing.

> In the early morning, the sun rose from the east, and the whole campus lit up.
> A new day had begun. The sound of reading aloud and singing fluttered in the air…

The entire class exploded with laughter before I could finish. My classmates laughed so loudly that the room rocked. What was wrong with my essay? I stood there, feeling confused, and I couldn't go on with my reading. I didn't know why my classmates were laughing. I looked at Lemin, Leping and Yisong, who all lowered their heads with embarrassment as if they had caused the trouble.

Teacher Ma laughed too. He said: "Huang Mingjiang, sit down please.

Now, class, stop laughing. Mingjiang has done a great job. His essay is good. Very concise language and vivid description. One suggestion for him though – 'flutter' could be replaced by 'fly'."

Everyone stopped laughing and listened quietly to Teacher Ma, whose comments and evaluations were reasonable, to be honest. I could see my classmates were convinced, and I gradually calmed down.

But I needed to know why my classmates had laughed. I went to see Teacher Ma after class, and he said: "I think it was mainly because of your mispronunciation."

Then, I realised why I had made a fool of myself. Instead of *shu sheng* ('the sound of reading aloud'), I had said *zhu sheng* ('the grunt of a pig'). No wonder everyone in the classroom doubled up with laughter!

I couldn't really be blamed for this. Our village was in a remote area that was very hard to reach. In the early 1980s, we had no roads and no running water, let alone electricity. Without electricity, things that are quite common nowadays, like TVs and computers, were beyond our imagination. At that time, we had never seen or heard of any of them! The only access we had to the outside world was listening to the radio. Households in our village were not well off, and the number of families who had a radio could be counted on the fingers of one hand. It had been quite a few years since Mandarin Chinese was promoted nationwide, but in our daily life we mostly spoke Zhuang and had few chances to be in contact with standard Mandarin. That we could understand it was an achievement in itself. The teacher in our village school could speak a little Mandarin in the classroom, and it was from him that we learned.

The most horrible thing was our academic performance. We were far behind our classmates. In the modern vernacular, we had already lost at the starting line.

Just think about it: there were ten or so students in our village school, with one teacher and four forms in one classroom. During each class period, this one teacher had four years together. In other words, in one lesson, only a quarter of the class time could be given to us; this was ten minutes or so. There were times when these ten minutes could not be guaranteed either, such as when the teacher was giving us a lecture. And what could he do when he found some older students were making trouble or the younger students were crying? If he didn't settle it quickly, the whole classroom would be in a mess.

In contrast, students in Tuanlong School were in a class with their peers in the same year group, and their teachers would be able to focus on imparting knowledge. So we were far behind! Put it this way: our four class periods equalled one of theirs, which meant we only had one year of study during the four years of primary school education. That was our so-called multi-form teaching. We all knew that if we wanted to catch up with the other students, we had no choice but to work hard and make up for the lost three years.

But that's easier said than done. The gap between our classmates and us was huge, and we often felt utterly exhausted and helpless.

The deadliest blow was the periodical test. That was our first test since joining Tuanlong School, and it was a disaster. All of us failed in Chinese and maths. For those who failed, the teachers would write the grades in red ink, so we said we got wounded in battle and we bled. Our names were ranked first, second, third and fourth in our class – starting from the bottom of the list, of course! On our way home after class, none of us was in the mood to talk. We each grabbed a small wooden stick and whipped the small trees along the road to vent our anger.

When we got back to our village, we agreed to keep the terrible results a secret from our parents for the time being.

12

HARVESTING THE BLACK OLIVES

The black olives on the trees were all ripe. It was harvest time. At the edge of our village, there were six tall black olive trees planted by my dad's second uncle.

I had never seen my second great-uncle. He died many years before. Of course, he had never seen me because when he was still alive I hadn't been born into this world yet; even my dad was just a child at that time.

My dad told me that when he was still a little boy, Second Great-Uncle had been quite old. He was a little old man and remained single his whole life. He had a hunched back that was so severe that it made his chin almost touch his knees. All day long, he would hang around with a dung basket in his arms, picking up pig and cattle manure to be used as fertiliser for all the fruit trees he had planted.

Dad told me that Second Great-Uncle was addicted to planting fruit trees. He planted longan, grapefruit, almonds, loquat and lychees – any type of fruit tree. He wanted to change our village into a large garden. He had no children or grandchildren, and he said all the villagers were his offspring. He wanted to make sure that everyone could have fresh fruit to eat all year round.

Later, Second Great-Uncle thought of planting black olive trees so that we could have the best black olives to eat. We loved black olives. There was a saying in our village: "You don't need salt and oil when you bake pork with black olives." As soon as the black olives matured, it was time to harvest them.

After the harvest, Dad would bring home our share. Mum would cook them first in water. Then, she would take a thin thread, bite hard at one end and hold the other end tightly in her right hand. She tied this around the middle of a cooked black olive and, with a light pull, the thin thread would cut the fruit into two halves. She would then hold the fruit at the two pointed tips and bend it slightly. The hard stone of the fruit fell out, leaving two halves of the empty shell. Mum would then cook some taro or potatoes shaped like a leg of beef, mash them and season. After that, she would stuff each shell with the mashed fillings, placed the stuffed olive into a jar, press hard and seal it tight. A couple of weeks later, a delicious olive dish would be ready to enjoy!

But it was not easy to plant black olive trees. Olive saplings were only available in Shengzhi Village, and the trip there and back was more than sixty *li* of mountain road. Also, it was not easy for saplings to survive. Second Great-Uncle planted some young trees, but they died soon afterwards. So, he planted some again, but they died too.

"He was determined to grow black olive trees even though they died and died again!" said my dad.

I was wondering why he hadn't asked the young men to get the saplings since it was such a long journey.

My dad said: "Well, the young men in our village offered to go because they didn't want Second Great-Uncle to work so hard, but he just wouldn't listen. He always wanted to do things his own way, and he couldn't feel at ease unless he went to get the saplings himself. The olive saplings kept dying, but he returned to Shengzhi Village again and again without becoming discouraged."

An image of an old man emerged in my mind – an old man whose chin almost touched his knees as he walked alone on the long mountain road to Shengzhi Village. No matter how tiring and hard the journey was, he managed to move on unswervingly, just to give the people in the village a chance to eat olives. In my mind, Second Great-Uncle was amazing. He was a huge mountain standing in front of me. I couldn't help admiring him and said: "What a good man Second Great-Uncle was. Life for him was so hard."

Dad said: "Right! We told him this when we were young. Can you guess how he answered us? He said, 'Living in this world, you can't be afraid of working hard!' He even sang *shan'ge* for us at that time."

I was surprised. "With such a hunched back, Second Great-Uncle could sing *shan'ge*?"

"I was surprised too," said Dad. "An old man with a hunched back who planted fruit trees in our village could sing *shan'ge*. He really did know how to sing. He hummed in a low voice, sounding aged and hoarse, but it was very pleasant to the ears."

I replied excitedly: "Dad, please sing Second Great-Uncle's *shan'ge* for me."

"OK. I've learned it by heart, and I'm sure you'll never forget it after you hear it."

With his eyes half closed, my dad began to sing the song softly. Soft as his voice was, it still sounded bold and powerful.

> *Liao luo wei,*
> *How many turns has the Bachi River taken?*
> *How many shoals of green bamboo carps can swim across it?*
> *Why should we be afraid of heavy labour on the farmland?*
> *Good boys dare to swim against the current.*

I listened and was completely transfixed. I said to my dad: "Second Great-Uncle's *shan'ge* is really good. I've memorised it already!"

Dad said: "He had more. I remember saying to him, 'Second Uncle, is it really difficult to plant a black olive tree?' He said it was not a big deal – if he should fail the first time, he would do it again. If it didn't work the second time, he would try a third time! I told him he had actually failed for a third time, but he said he would go on for a fourth time and a fifth time!" As my dad told me this, he began to sing to me again:

> *Liao luo wei,*
> *If you want to eat honey, raise bees;*
> *If you want to eat delicious fruits, plant trees.*
> *As long as you have an iron will,*
> *Young trees are sure to grow tall, offering cool shade.*

When we arrived at the foot of the black olive trees, most of the adults and children in our village were already there. Lemin, Leping and Yisong also came. Everyone was so happy – it was as if they were celebrating a festival.

Dad and dozens of young men climbed up the trees like monkeys, two or three of them standing on one tree and holding a long bamboo pole. As they waved the pole to hit clusters of the bright black olives, the ripe ones left the branches and flew down to the ground like hailstones. Elders, women and noisy children, who were laughing and shouting like birds, picked up the black pearl-like fruit and put them into paddy baskets, which gradually filled up amid our laughter. The fruit on the trees gradually disappeared while the paddy baskets on the ground were filled and looked like small mountains.

Someone began singing *liaoluo*, and I immediately recognised my mum's voice. When she was halfway through the first line, the other women joined her. Sweet and silvery singing flew from under the trees and floated in the forests. I looked up and found that the tall and flourishing black olive trees seemed to be growing.

> *Liao luo yi luo,*
> One generation plants trees whose fruit another generation enjoys.
> Delicious black olive fruits,
> The descendants will never forget.
> The spirit of Second Great-Uncle will be passed on forever.

The men cheered loudly, and we followed suit.

When Mum walked over to a paddy basket, pouring the olives she had picked and carried in her blouse, I asked: "Mum, did Second Great-Uncle eat the black olives he himself had planted?"

Mum shook her head with a grateful and admiring look on her face. She said: "He was very old when he was planting the olive trees. It takes at least ten years for an olive tree to grow, bloom and yield fruit. When I married your dad, these olive trees had just started to bloom for the first year. At that time, Second Great-Uncle had been gone for many years. According to your father, when he planted the trees, he knew that he wouldn't have the chance to eat the fruit. He also said that even if it should blossom and yield fruit at once, he would not be able to eat it because all of his teeth had fallen out. He had planted these olive trees for us and for the future generations."

My dad was responsible for taking care of these fruit trees, as well as for harvesting and fruit distribution. These tasks had been given to him by Second Great-Uncle before he died. He also said that when my dad grew old, a young man must be assigned to do this work and new trees must be planted when the old ones could no longer yield fruit. In this way, people in the village would have delicious olives to eat for generations.

Dad had done this work for many years, and he knew how to do it well. He shouted happily: "It's time to divide the fruit!" Holding a large bowl, he gave two portions to everyone – men and women, young and old. Those who participated in the fruit collection would have an extra portion.

Leping had already taken off his shirt and spread it on the ground. He put his share of the fruit on the shirt, tied it tightly and carried it over his shoulder, saying: "Now we don't need to worry about our lunch at school."

Lemin said: "There's no need to share our dishes any more. Everyone has the same!"

I said: "I guess we still need to share to see whose mum cooks the best!"

My mum and the other women heard my words. They smiled knowingly at each other and said: "Look, the kids are pushing us to have a cooking competition!"

I knew the olive dishes we would bring to school for lunch were sure to be sweet and delicious.

13
LEARN FROM SECOND GREAT-UNCLE'S EXAMPLE

On Sunday, my parents and I sat under the bamboo-shoot lamp cutting olives after dinner. The olives had already been cooked in a large pot. Mum was cutting them quickly with one end of a silk thread between her teeth and the other end in her hand. The olives she had cut soon piled up in front of her. My dad and I hurriedly picked up the fruit and pulled out the hard stones.

After being busy with this work for a while, I finally had to tell my parents about my periodical test.

I said: "Dad, Mum, we had a periodical test yesterday, and we all failed!"

Dad looked at me and said with a smile: "I know."

I was surprised. We had decided not to tell our parents. Who had let the cat out of the bag? "Dad, how did you know this?" I asked.

"You told me!"

"Me?"

"Yes, your face told me everything!"

I stuck out my tongue. My dad was so smart – he could see through me!

"How about your scores then?" my dad asked with concern.

"I didn't pass, so it doesn't matter what scores I got. There's no difference between my scores and a zero."

"How could it be the same as getting a zero? Tell me, what did you get?"

"Fifty-eight for Chinese, and fifty-one for maths."

Dad said: "For Chinese, you only need two more points, while it's nine for maths. That's not the same as getting a zero. Zero means nothing, but you've achieved something. It's not bad, and you've worked hard."

I said disappointedly: "I did work hard but look at my result. We don't know how to do it and we're losing confidence. It's so humiliating whenever we think that we are the last four at the bottom."

"Oh, the last four?"

I nodded with embarrassment. "We all feel we owed you something for the lunch you have cooked for us."

My dad chortled – he seemed to be happy about it. So did my mum. I didn't understand why they were reacting this way. I just felt like crying.

Dad asked: "What are you boys going to do?"

"We don't know." We had no idea. We had been thinking it over for a long time but still had no way out.

Dad asked: "How many periodical tests have you had?"

"This was the first one! We all mucked it up!"

Dad said: "Mucked it up? You did anything but that. When Second Great-Uncle planted black olive trees for the first time, all the saplings died, which was indeed a zero score, a real failure. You got fifty-eight in Chinese, which in a sense means half of the saplings you have planted have survived!"

Looking at my dad, I felt something had struck me suddenly.

"Second Great-Uncle was a little sad, but he was not at all discouraged. His method was to walk dozens of *li* to get saplings and plant them again. He failed again the second time but he tried a third time. When he failed at the third attempt, he went on with the fourth. Eventually, six black olive trees survived. Now, all the villagers can eat delicious olives. If Second Great-Uncle had given up, we would have never had the chance to see the six giant black olive trees weighed down with fruit."

As he said this, Dad began to hum Second Great-Uncle's *shan'ge*.

> *Liao luo wei,*
> *How many turns has the Bachi River taken?*
> *How many shoals of green bamboo carps can swim across it?*
> *Why should we be afraid of heavy labour on the farmland?*
> *Good boys dare to swim against the current.*

Mum sang along, and so did I.

After we had finished singing, Mum smiled and said: "In our family, the bull mooed and so did the calf!"

"Definitely! Dad's *jiate* sounds more and more wonderful. I need to learn from him."

Dad said to me: "Well, in my view, you're only two points away from sixty. That's forty-two away from a hundred. Not a big gap. Don't be afraid. Let's work out a way. How about trying again like Second Great-Uncle? You four are big boys. You can find a way forward, can't you?"

On our way to school the next day, we were still in a heavy mood. There was no laughter and no singing. We walked silently in the darkness, crushed and crestfallen like defeated roosters. When we arrived at Genma Ridge, the stars were blinking in the sky. It was still early, so I said: "Let's take a break. We have enough time."

We sat on some rocks, staring at the stars and listening to the choir of crickets. Occasionally, some deep hoots came from the owls in the woods and we knew they were busy working before dawn.

I was the first one to speak. "I've told my scores to my parents."

Almost at the same time, Lemin, Leping and Yisong said they had done that too. We could never conceal anything from our parents. The periodical test was such an important matter, it was impossible for us to hide it from them.

Our families all knew the results, and none of them had scolded us. They hoped that we could try again like my second great-uncle.

Lemin said: "I just can't understand why we did so poorly though – we worked so hard."

Leping said: "I think I just lost my head completely. Before the test, I could answer all the maths questions, but once in the test, my mind went blank and I was sweating all over. Everything went wrong!"

Yisong said: "I think you have no confidence in yourself."

Leping was a little annoyed and retorted: "And you have confidence, do you? Why did you fail all the subjects then?"

Yisong replied: "I really didn't understand those questions in the test. I trembled uncontrollably when I read the questions, and my hands were unable to hold my pencil."

I said: "I've been thinking about why we are so far behind our classmates.

We didn't realise what we should have learned before we came to Tuanlong School. At our village school, with no one to compare us with, we were unaware of the difference. Our teacher couldn't teach us much, so we learned less. Compared with our classmates, we showed our true colours. My dad is right. This is what we really are."

Leping sighed: "What a waste of my strong body. It seems so hard for us to keep up with them."

Yisong said: "Yes, it's very difficult. I'm scared just thinking about this."

I said: "Difficult as it is, we must never give up. Wouldn't it have been more difficult for Mahuai to carry mountains back to our home town? Wouldn't it have been more difficult for Second Great-Uncle to plant black olive trees for the village?"

Lemin said: "My dad said everyone has to face difficulties in life. Our problem is nothing – a piece of cake."

I agreed. "Right, we should learn from Second Great-Uncle and never waver."

I shared my thoughts with them. I said we were no more stupid than anyone else. We were far behind the others because we hadn't learned well in the past. That is to say, we didn't have a solid foundation, and this had been holding us back. That's why we seemed to understand everything our teachers said in class, but we were thrown into confusion when we needed to use what we had learned before. To catch up with the others, we first of all had to make up for the knowledge that they had acquired previously.

Leping shouted: "Do we have to bone up on all that?"

"Definitely!" I said. "Let's learn from Second Great-Uncle walking dozens of *li* to fetch saplings and plant them again!"

So we made a decision. We had to catch up and be unafraid of hardships and difficulties.

We started our plan that very evening. Everyone came to my home on time, and we sat around the bright bamboo-shoot lamp. We finished that day's assignment first. Whenever someone had a question that involved some knowledge from before the fifth year, we four would recall what we had learned, check our old textbooks and review it. We called it "mending the hole", and we tried to solve any problems we encountered on the very same day. By doing this, the person who was having difficulties would get a quick solution, and those who helped would also gain a deeper understanding.

Although this took more time, we were all happy to do it because we could not only help our friends but also improve ourselves.

When we had finished that day's homework and reviewed it together, we set out to study the things we needed to know.

We agreed to start with maths on that first night.

"Let's start with lesson one of our maths textbook from the first term of year one," I said, taking out my old textbook.

Yisong took out his crumpled book from his bag, but Lemin and Leping didn't move. Seeing my enquiring look, Leping stammered: "I've searched for it for a long time. It might have been dragged away by the mice to build their den."

Lemin said: "I just flipped through it. I don't think there's any need for us to go over it."

I said: "It's better to start from the very beginning in case we missed something. OK, let's begin. Lesson one – numbers from one to ten."

We all laughed.

"We are fifth years. Is there anyone who can't count from one to ten?" Lemin said.

"What a low IQ we would have if we couldn't do it," Yisong said.

Leping said: "I don't remember having this lesson in class."

I laughed too and said: "Of course we don't have such a low IQ. But shall we check it through according to the syllabus? We should never let a single problem escape. I'll read on, and if everyone feels there's no problem, we can pass. So do you have any questions about lesson one?"

"Pass!" Everyone shouted with a smile.

"Lesson two, addition and subtraction within ten…"

"Pass!" Still laughing, everyone was in high spirits.

"Pass!"

"Pass!"

There were no problems with the maths from the first term of the first year.

It was the same for the second term of the first year.

Although we could laugh happily now, I knew that we might not be able to laugh at all in the evenings ahead.

The second evening was allocated to Chinese.

Everyone brought their textbook. For Chinese, we could not simply give a 'pass' to it like we did with maths. We had to do dictation in turn, with one reading aloud and the other three writing it down. We planned to work hard and memorise all the texts we had learned before we became fifth years – all of the characters and expressions.

We knew it was not a smart method, but clumsy birds have to start flying early. We believed we would make progress!

14

'SHU' NOT 'ZHU'

One day, Teacher Ma called us four to the staff room and said: "Huang Mingjiang, you wrote a good essay last time, but because your mother language is Zhuang, you couldn't pronounce the Chinese correctly. I hope we can all work together to overcome this difficulty. Do you think you can do it?"

We looked at each other and answered in unison: "Yes, we do!"

It was exactly what we wanted to do. We spoke Mandarin Chinese with strong Zhuang accents, which we were unaware of in our village because there was no one pointing it out. Now, in our new school, compared with our classmates, it stood out so obviously that we felt ashamed and couldn't lift our heads. We talked less and less. Our classmates called it 'Chouqing Mandarin' – a very stiff and immature dialect of Nanning City. At first, we were angry at this, but on reflection we felt it was actually a fair comment. We mispronounced *shu* ('book') as *zhu* ('pig'), and this would make people laugh their heads off. We did want to improve, but we didn't know where we were going wrong or what we should do. We also knew that their laughter was harmless, although we still felt sad.

Teacher Ma said: "It's mainly because you haven't learned Chinese Pinyin correctly. Why do you pronounce *shu* as *zhu*? Because you have read the initial consonant 'sh' as 'zh', and it's the same when you read *zhao* as *shao*. And when you confuse *kou* with *gou* it's because you're reading 'k' as 'g'. There are few or no such sounds in the Zhuang language, and that's why you sound so different when you pronounce Chinese Pinyin. You all have to practise Chinese Pinyin first. Practise more and overcome this difficulty."

"Now, read after me," said Teacher Ma, as he began to teach us how to read initial consonants.

After going through this twice, Teacher Ma said: "It's a little difficult for one person to remember all of them at once. Let's divide them into groups, and each of you can memorise five at first. Then, you can learn from each other later. Huang Mingjiang, you take the first six. Wei Tianmin, the following five belong to you. Qin Hanping, you can have the next five. And you take the last five, Li Yisong. Now, read after me, twice."

We read after Teacher Ma twice, and each of us memorised our given consonants. "I've prepared some characters that you often mispronounce," said Teacher Ma, plucking a sheet of paper from his teaching materials. We gathered around him.

"*Piao* is read as *biao*, the initial consonant 'p' being read as 'b'. *Tong* is read as *dong*, *tai* as *dai*, and *tian* as *dian*, the initial consonant 't' being read as 'd'. *Shu* is read as *zhu*, the initial consonant 'sh' being read as 'zh'. *Cong* is read as *xiong*, the initial consonant 'c' being read as 'x'. *Qing* is read as *xing*, the initial consonant 'q' being read as 'x'. *Kan* is read as *gan*, and *kou* as *gou*, the initial consonant 'k' being read as 'g'. Look, when you can't pronounce 'k' and 'sh', the expression *kou tou biao da* ('oral expression') would be pronounced *gou tou biao da* ('dog head expression'), and *shu mian hui bao* ('written report') becomes *zhu mian hui bao* ('pig face report')."

We couldn't help but laugh until our sides ached.

Biting his lip to keep from laughing, Teacher Ma said: "Hurry up and work harder. First of all, pronounce the following sounds correctly – po, te, ke, ci, shi."

Then Teacher Ma taught us those initial consonants again, elaborating on their characteristics and the place of articulation of each sound. Indeed, we didn't have those sounds in the Zhuang language. When we read after Teacher Ma, our tongues were stiff and out of control. We were still pronouncing *kou tou* as *gou tou*, and *shu mian* as *zhu mian*, but it was impossible for us to change it at once.

"It's very natural considering you boys have practised for such a short time!" Teacher Ma encouraged us, his eyes full of care and love. "If you practise every day, I believe you can master all of them, without any question."

After class that day, we recited those consonants as we walked all the way back. We concentrated so hard that the ten-*li* mountain road seemed to become shorter, and we arrived at our village even before we realised it.

We scattered away and ran back to our homes. There was still a lot of housework for us to help with.

Reciting Pinyin on our way back home was really fun. When we worked together, it was easier for us, and it lasted longer in our minds. So we hit upon an idea immediately: why didn't we just make the best use of our evenings? Yes, we could use the ten-*li* journey to study Chinese.

After that, we made the most of this time by reciting texts we had learned, especially ancient poems and prose. We recited all the way back, sometimes playing solitaire, that is, one of us recited the first line of a poem, then the next person went on with the second line. If he failed to go on, the third person took over. If no one could recite the next line, we would switch on our torches and check it in our textbook. In this way, it would leave a deep impression on us. After the game, we four would recite it together once again, thinking about whether there was still something we didn't understand, whether there was a character we couldn't write, who the author was and in which dynasty the author lived. When all these questions were answered, we would shout together:

"Pass!"

If we still had time on our journey, we would recite one more.

Sometimes, one of us recited, and the other three listened attentively, trying to spot mistakes, which in a sense required all of us to have the ability to recite. This method was used by us to recite texts other than poems. Later, we even recited texts that we were not required to recite.

For us, being familiar with and reciting texts was extremely important. In the past, we had only spoken the Zhuang language, whose grammar was a lot different from Mandarin Chinese. With these texts as a foundation, it became much easier for us to choose words and expressions when we made sentences.

The sound of texts being recited and the enthusiastic shouts of "Pass!" stayed in the mountains and rivers of our home town as well as in our hearts.

15
RESCUING A MOTHER FOX

Early one morning on our way to school, we were reciting *The Willow*, a classic poem written by He Zhizhang in the Tang Dynasty.

I began with the first line: "*Bi yu zhuang cheng yi shu gao.*" ("Emerald fashioned into a tall tree.")

Leping went on with the second: "*Wan tiao chui xia lü si tiao.*" ("Hung with a myriad of silk braids of green.")

Lemin continued: "*Bu zhi xi ye shui cai chu?*" ("Who tailored the dainty leaves?")

Yisong finished the last line: "*Er yue chun feng si jian dao.*" ("The cutting wind of early spring.")

I felt there was something wrong and asked: "Why does *tiao* appear twice in the second line? One character would not be used twice in an ancient poem."

Leping argued: "There are two – I remember clearly that the second one has a different constructive part."

Lemin said: "Yes, I remember it too."

I said: "No wonder it sounds a little strange. Leping, the second one, with the different constructive part, is not *tiao* – it should be pronounced *tao*, meaning lace or a flat ribbon. *Lü si tao* refers to lace or a ribbon braided with green silk thread. Also, *tao* and *dao* rhyme better."

Leping said: "I made a mistake. Yes, it should be *Wan tiao chui xia lü si tao*."

I said: "Let's recite it together."

We recited the poem aloud again.

Leping said: "I think the character *bi* ('green') is a little difficult to write."

I suddenly thought of the riddle for the character *bi*. I forgot who had told me this, but it was very clever.

I announced: "Listen. I have a riddle for you, and I'm sure you'll remember the character *bi* for your whole life after you listen to it. It goes like this – *yi shi yi, jiu shi jiu, wu dou you wu dou* ('one ten one, ninety-nine, five *dou* plus five *dou*')."

Without any clues, they couldn't work out the answer, no matter how hard they racked their brains.

"Well, here's the answer. The character *bi* has three constructive parts: *wang*, *bai* and *shi*. *Yi shi yi* forms the character *wang* when their strokes are put together. We will get ninety-nine if we subtract one from one hundred, so *bai* (when written as a Chinese character, it means 'white') is ninety-nine. Five *dou* plus five *dou* is ten *dou*, while in the past, ten *dou* equalled one *dan*, so we have the constructive part *shi* (*shi* and *dan* are homographs in Chinese) of the character *bi*. What do you think about the riddle? It's a clever one, isn't it?"

They all thought about it and decided it was indeed a good one. In the darkness, Leping drew the strokes of *bi* with his finger and said: "Amazing! I'll never forget it."

Yisong said: "The line *Er yue chun feng si jian dao* ('The cutting wind of early spring') has given me a strange idea. My understanding is that it's still chilly in February. When the spring wind blows, it bites your ears as if scissors are cutting your ears – very painful! That's why we have *Er yue chun feng si jian dao*."

We were very surprised that Yisong could have such a unique understanding!

Lemin said: "But the third line is *Bu zhi xi ye shui cai chu?* ('Who tailored the dainty leaves?') so the last line is the answer to the third line. It tells us the spring wind in February tailors the dainty leaves like a pair of scissors. Yisong, your understanding is therefore definitely not right."

I agreed with Lemin. I said: "Yisong, it seems your understanding could be all right when the line *Er yue chun feng si jian dao* is taken into consideration alone, but when we put it into the context of the whole poem, what you just said makes little sense."

Wow, we didn't know when we had acquired the ability to think about questions like these on our ten-*li* mountain road journey, and even make such a clear and logical analysis!

"The fox is coming again!" Lemin uttered in a low cry.

Yisong was not afraid this time. He said: "I know it can't be a tiger."

We stopped still. The fox was sitting on a ridge not far from where we were, its eyes appearing faint green as they reflected light from the torch. It seemed to be very interested in our discussion. It probably realised that we were looking at it, so it stood up, stretched its body and, in an unhurried manner, ran down the mountain ridge, which was the left leg of The Immortal Watching the Moon. The fox quickly disappeared into the dense forest along the Bachi River.

This fox was our old friend – we had seen it several times before. It would be impossible for us to see it if we arrived there too late or too early because it would always be there at the same time. The green light would appear before us and go down the mountain ridge.

"Why does it always run to the river?"

"It's probably going back home!"

"Foxes like to go out at night. It must have been busy looking for food the whole night."

"But it doesn't look very tired, does it?"

But we didn't continue our discussion about the fox for a long time because we began to recite another poem, *Happy Rain on a Spring Night*:

> *Good rain knows the right time;*
> *It will fall when spring comes.*
> *With wind it steals in the night;*
> *Mute, it moistens each thing.*
> *Over wild lanes, a dark cloud spreads;*
> *In a boat, a lantern looms.*
> *Dawn sees saturated reds;*
> *The town is heavy with blooms.*

This poem was written by Du Fu, the great poet of the Tang Dynasty, and could be recited quite smoothly. It was easy to understand as well. Some things in the poem were still worth memorising, such as *nai* ('will'), *yejing* ('wild lanes'), *ju* ('all') and *hongshi* ('saturated reds'). We liked the word *qian* ('to slip into stealthily') best. We went diving in the river, and this was always done quietly, which could also be considered stealth-like. Dr Fu had chosen the perfect word here. If he had used *chui* ('blow'), the poem would be much less vivid.

Spring Rain brought us to the school that hadn't woken up yet.

After school, we thought of the fox, our old friend we had met many times, so we decided to visit its home.

We first found the position where it used to stand, ran down the mountain ridge it used to go down, dived into the woods along the river and then scattered away to look for it separately. We searched carefully in the woods, sweating all over, but we couldn't see it anywhere. Instead, we startled a few colourful pheasants and some spotted partridges. In a panic, they crackled and flew across the river.

We became fond of this fox. After school the next day, we continued our search.

Lemin said: "This time, we should cover as much ground as possible. Brother Jiang and Yisong, check the east. Leping and I will search the west. We must find it even if we have to dig three feet deep!" He borrowed the line from some dialogue in a film.

Yisong agreed: "Yes, dig three feet deep to find its den! It must be in the woods beside the river."

To be honest, we had no idea where foxes made their homes – on trees, in hollow trees or hidden in clumps of grass. We just searched everywhere, aimlessly.

I thought about it for a while and said: "Foxes are said to be very sly. In stories, wolves are never a match for them. I suspect it intended to lead us in the wrong direction when it ran towards the river. Its den is not beside the river at all. Otherwise, why couldn't we find any traces of it yesterday? I think we should search right here!"

We all agreed to try.

There were pastures in this place – no tall and big trees but some low bushes, clusters of hazelnuts, wild peaches and Indian gooseberries. Above the mountain ridge, there was a large pit in the near distance – a cave-in to be exact – where dense thickets of shrubs flourished. It was the very navel of the immortal, in the opposite direction to the river where the fox ran each time.

Yisong and I went to check the pit together.

We approached it quietly and looked down from the edge. The slanting sunlight filtered through the trees onto the bottom of the pit, freckling the ground with innumerable little spangles of light. At first, we could see nothing. When our eyes adapted to the light inside the pit, we found there were a few small balls rolling on the ground. Yisong made a gesture and whispered to me: "Brother Jiang, there seem to be a few puppies in the pit."

In a second, those small balls disappeared. They were alarmed and hid themselves immediately. The pit resumed its silence.

I asked Yisong to stay there watching while I clung to some tree roots along the inside edge of the pit and descended slowly to the bottom. There was a small horizontal hole in the bottom, and a suffocating, funky smell attacked my nostrils from its entrance. I hurriedly climbed back to the top and told Yisong that what we just saw were not puppies but fox cubs. The fox had built its den in the pit!

Lemin and Leping hurried over when they saw Yisong's gesture. As they were running to us, they asked: "Have you found it?"

I pointed at the pit, which was flourishing with dense shrubs, and I whispered: "Just inside the pit!" Then, I pulled them aside in case we might alarm the cubs.

Yisong said: "She's a mother fox!"

Leping said: "No wonder she would always lead us to the river. She's protecting her cubs."

Lemin exclaimed: "What a clever mother fox! She thought of building her den inside the navel of the immortal."

Yisong added: "I saw the baby foxes. They were rolling on the ground like some meatballs – so cute!"

Lemin asked hurriedly: "How many?"

Yisong said: "I saw three of them. Brother Jiang climbed down to the bottom, so he must know better than me."

I replied with embarrassment: "When I got to the bottom, the baby foxes all hid in the hole. I didn't hear a single sound, let alone see them."

We decided not to let anyone know this in case it might disturb the mother fox and bring her family anxiety, or even trouble.

From then on, we would go to visit the fox family after school and stay beside their den for a while. We knelt beside the edge of the pit, staring at the bottom quietly, our chins in our hands. We saw five cubs at most. They gleefully romped around in the freckled sunshine, ears pricking up, ready to hide in the den as soon as they should feel something wrong, leaving no chance for us to find where they were. We never saw the mother fox. We guessed she must have been busy finding food all night and she was now taking a rest inside the den or was feeding her cubs.

It was in the morning darkness that we would see the mother fox. The green lights let us know she was there. She would sit there looking at us pensively for a while and then run towards the Bachi River, along the ridge, as if nothing had happened.

We all looked at each other with a smile of understanding. We wanted to say to her: "Mother Fox, stop cheating us. We know where your family is, and we often go to visit your home! Mother Fox, don't worry. We'll never hurt you."

The first time we saw the mother fox run to her den was on a morning a few days later. We noticed the green lights of her eyes seemed a bit farther away than usual, moving slowly towards her den, and occasionally we could hear slight tinkling sounds of pieces of metal striking each other.

We ran towards the sound in a hurry and found the mother fox was struggling on the ground. She looked at us helplessly, fangs bared and growling angrily. It turned out that her right front leg was caught by a metal mouse trap attached to an iron chain. The mother fox was running back to her den with the metal trap. At that time, the iron chain was caught on a small bare tree root, and she couldn't drag it anymore. She curled up and gasped there.

We were shocked and saddened. Who had set the trap? The mother fox was caught, so we had to rescue her and get her out of trouble.

But the mother fox was fully alert and wouldn't allow us to approach her.

"Mother Fox, don't be afraid. We are helping you," Yisong said as he moved to her slowly.

The mother fox growled. She hunched her body and was ready to pounce at us. It was very dangerous to get close to her at that moment. We wanted to help her, but we didn't know what to do.

Lemin was quick-witted. He said: "Let's find a V-shaped branch to control the mother fox so that she can't move. Then, we can loosen the trap."

Leping said: "I know where we can get a V-shaped stem."

We all thought of it as well. Someone had heaped a pile of dry wood, on which long wooden sticks were placed, nearby. Some of the sticks at the top were V-shaped.

Yisong said: "Brother Ping, I'll go with you."

Very soon, they were back with two sticks.

Lemin said: "Pardon us for interrupting you, Mother Fox." As he said this, he pressed the stick on the mother fox's neck, and I pressed the other one on her belly. The mother fox wanted to struggle against us but was held down.

Yisong walked over, trying to step on the trap. I shouted: "Watch out! The fox has very sharp claws! Take care not to be scratched by her."

Leping said: "Yisong, let me try. I'm wearing high-ankle sports shoes, so the fox's claws are not a threat."

As he said this, he pressed hard on the triggering mechanism with the tip of his shoes, and the spring-loaded iron trap swung open. He grabbed the iron chain, pulled it with a jerk and the trap left the mother fox's leg.

It was a small iron trap, and it had caught the mother fox close to her claw. She was not badly hurt, but she bled a little. The blood turned dry and caked the hair on her foot. We quickly got some young peach and hazelnut leaves, chewed them and applied them to the fox's wound. Then, we wrapped the wound with my lunch mug cover – a fig leaf – and bound it tightly with the rope I used to tie my lunch mug. The mother fox was very quiet at that moment. She was lying there, panting, with her belly rising and falling, allowing us to take care of her wound without making any trouble.

"Listen to me carefully," I said. "Let go of the stick after the count of three. One, two, three…"

Lemin and I lifted the stick at the same time. The mother fox stood up, took a look at us and dashed away towards her home at once. She limped and turned back to look at us again as she ran a few steps. Then, she disappeared into the woods of the immortal's navel.

We all sighed with relief and continued our journey. There was no cover for my lunch mug, so I had to protect it with my hands to keep the food from spilling out.

In the darkness, Yisong sighed: "The first thing the mother fox thought about was her babies."

I thought she must be feeding her babies as she was telling them about her adventure. It was likely that she might sing the fox's *liaoluo* if foxes had one.

16
BRINGING A CHICKEN TO THE FOX

We brought the iron trap back to the village. We had to return it to its master, and the most important thing was to tell the villagers that a mother fox who had five lovely cubs had been caught in it. We should never hurt her again.

We went door-to-door to explain the situation to each household.

Finally, we found the owner of the iron trap, who turned out to be my neighbour, Uncle Bofu. When we entered his house, he was cooking supper. He recognised the trap before we opened our mouths.

"It's my iron trap. How did it come to you?" he asked us with a puzzled look.

I told him what had happened.

Uncle Bofu said: "Luckily, you boys have saved the mother fox. It would have been very difficult for the cubs to survive if the mother fox had died. If so, my sins would be great! You're all good boys to behave so kindly. Thank you so much!"

Uncle Bofu was quite sincere and very grateful to us. It was not surprising that people in our village all loved to do good deeds. Uncle Bofu took the trap and said: "You, iron trap! Why did you catch a mother fox instead of those mice? I can't keep you anymore!"

As he said this, he lifted an axe and smashed the trap into a useless wreck.

There was a story about mice in our village.

In a place named Chongbo, there was a sweet potato field. Wild animals, who loved to loot crops, developed a fondness for a sweet potato field because there were only root crops left after grains had been harvested. Pheasants and partridges saw that clearly from the sky, and they made themselves the guests in that field. They were very disciplined, coming during the day, spotting a sweet potato under the ground, scratching it out of the earth and returning to peck it each day. They would not go and find a second one until they finished the first.

Field voles, however, were very annoying. They were night thieves. After they found a sweet potato field, they would burrow into the ground, dig out a long tunnel and eat up all the sweet potatoes in the field without leaving any trace on the surface. These field voles were quite large fellows, one adult vole weighing about a Chinese pound. They ate a lot, and two or three adult voles would ruin a sweet potato field.

Besides protecting crops, there was another reason for Uncle Bofu to catch mice – he would bring them to the market in Baodong after he caught them. Some of the people in our village liked to eat field voles. They often claimed that one vole equalled three chickens. Unlike rats, field voles only fed on plants in the mountains, and they were pretty clean; their fur looked shiny black. It was no wonder they became a favourite to eat. Uncle Bofu's voles would always sell for a good price.

Uncle Bofu explained: "I went to collect iron traps this morning and found one missing. After I checked it carefully, I found some fox footprints. I thought the fox had dragged away the vole caught by the trap. I even cursed the fox at that time. I said, 'You sly fox! Let's say no more about stealing my vole, but why did you take my iron trap away? You're just being unreasonable!' I searched nearby but couldn't find it. I had no choice but to give up. How could I know the trap had caught a fox instead of a vole? What's more, a mother fox with five cubs. I'm to blame for it. Voles don't have much strength, so I just tied the chain around the grass and it was done. No wonder the fox dragged it away!"

On our way to school the next morning, we didn't see the mother fox, who usually went out at night and returned home early in the morning.

After school in the afternoon, we went to check the pit. Kneeling on the edge, we looked down and saw the rear part of the mother fox lying on the ground. The five cubs crawled beside her and appeared quite weak. The mother's long tail wagged from time to time. We were greatly relieved to know she was still alive.

"I see, the mother fox has hurt her foot, so she is unable to go out to find food!" I said sadly.

Yisong said: "The cubs must be starving. Why else would they be crawling about on the ground?"

Lemin said: "We have got to find a way to help them."

"How about we save some food for them every day so that they won't get hungry anymore?" Leping said.

Everyone agreed.

I said: "Let's save one of our lunches, and we four can share the other three."

That night, I asked: "Mum, can you prepare extra food for me tomorrow? I want to save some for the wounded mother fox."

Mum said: "It's easy to prepare extra food for you, but foxes only eat meat. Will she be grateful for your kindness?"

Dad said: "Wild foxes don't eat rice. They only eat meat."

"Only meat?" An idea flashed through my mind. I said to Mum hurriedly: "We have some young roosters that haven't learned to crow. Could we take one to the mother fox? She is so helpless!"

Dad said: "We can, but these roosters are being kept for you to eat. If we give one to the mother fox, you're going to lose one."

We usually had very little meat at home, and I was looking forward to the day when those young roosters would grow up quickly and we would celebrate the holidays. My mouth watering, I swallowed and said: "I would rather eat less and help the mother fox through a hard time."

Mum said: "We're proud that our Lejiang has such a kind heart. But we don't know whether foxes accept food from a human being."

Dad said: "Let's have a try."

I jumped up and ran to the chicken coops. Dad helped me catch one of the young roosters and tied its feet with a rope.

I dared not take the chicken to the mountain in the dark at night-time on my own, so I invited Lemin, Leping and Yisong to come with me. We were long accustomed to walking on the mountain road in the early morning darkness, but we were a little afraid to do it at night. We didn't know why, and none of us spoke about it either. We tried to cheer ourselves up by singing a song as we walked, and we were definitely out of tune under those circumstances.

As we approached the pit, we stopped singing and turned off our torches. We moved closer, quietly, and hoped we would not disturb the family. The mother fox usually went out for food at night and came back early the next morning. Would she still be in her den tonight? We hoped she had been able to go out looking for food. I tied a big stone on the chicken's leg and put it into the pit quietly.

The next day when we were on the road to school, we didn't see the mother fox; normally, she would be coming home after finding food. We wanted to check the pit, but we eventually decided against it for fear that the torches might scare them. It was not until the afternoon, after we had been dismissed from school, that we dared to go to the pit to check what was going on. We found the stone we had used to tie the chicken was still there, but the chicken was gone. A few baby foxes were scampering inside the pit where chicken feathers were scattered around the bottom.

We knew the mother fox was in her den and she had eaten the young rooster we gave her.

I decided to bring her and her family one more chicken.

Lemin, Leping and Yisong were hesitant. I knew they felt too embarrassed to speak because they had fewer chickens and ducks in their homes.

I said: "It's only a few days since the mother fox got hurt by the trap, and she is still unable to look for food herself. If they don't have any food to eat tonight, they are going to suffer from hunger. But it seems there's nothing more we can do today."

Dad was very happy when he heard the mother fox had eaten the chicken. He said: "It's good news that the mother fox is willing to accept our help. Since there's no other way for the time being, let's give them one more chicken. It's worthwhile to save their family even if we lose two chickens."

Mum was a little reluctant, but eventually she agreed.

Then, Dad came up with a good idea. "Lejiang, it's Sunday tomorrow, isn't it? I suggest you boys catch fish. There are many big fish in the river, but they're difficult to catch because of the deep water. Small fish and shrimps hide in pools, and it would be better for you to catch them in the rice fields, especially the catfish. Catch as many as you can since it's easy to look after them at home. Then, you could take fish to the fox family a few times, and the fox family will have food every day."

The catfish Dad mentioned had four pairs of barbells and a pair of bony, sharp pectoral fins that contained venom, which was scary indeed. Once you were stung by its fins, it hurt badly. Catfish didn't have scales, and it was a hardy fish that could live as long as there was water. It tasted delicious, and we all liked to eat it.

On our way back home, after taking the chicken to the fox, I told my friends what my dad had said, and they immediately welcomed the idea. We four were experts at catching fish and shrimps in the rice fields. We decided to fish for a whole Sunday to prepare enough food for the mother fox and her family.

17

CATCHING FISH IN FORTY PADDY FIELD

We rose early every day to go to school, and we never got bored of it, but we were teenagers, and we still wanted to have a nice long lie-in on one day – namely Sunday. When Sunday came, our parents would not wake us up in the morning. They just let us sleep as long as we wanted.

But on this Sunday, we didn't want to sleep in. We set out very early in the morning and gathered at the edge of our village. We were going to catch fish for the mother fox and her family.

We were fully equipped and ready for the 'battle'. In our hands, we had basins to bail out the water. On our shoulders, we carried nets to sweep up the fish. Around our waists, we each hung a fishing rod with a container to hold the fish. There was no fish on the rods yet, but we did have some cooked sweet potatoes for our lunch.

In our village, the rice fields were all located between the mountains, paddy after paddy, tiered one after another, extending to the Bachi River. The place where the paddy fields connected with the river was called the plunge mouth.

Owing to the abundant mountain springs and numerous creeks, many of the paddy fields in our village were named '*baodong* fields' because they had enough water to survive the winter. The paddies of ascending terrace looked like clusters of precious mirrors surrounding our small village beside the

Bachi River; it was indeed a unique sight. The *baodong* paddies were rich in fish and shrimps. At any place in our paddy fields, as long as we dipped our hands deep into the soil, dug and turned the mud over, we were sure to catch some slippery loaches. Catching eels was our speciality. Walking on the field ridge and staring through the water at the mud in the field, we could immediately see whether eels were hiding inside the holes in the mud, and we knew their sizes as well. If there was one, we bent down and dug our right forefinger into the hole. The eel inside the hole would think that delicious food was coming and snap at it immediately. That's exactly what we wanted it to do. Holding it tight between the thumb and the forefinger, we would drag the eel out of its hole and throw it into our fishing net. When the eels found they had been cheated, they could do nothing but struggle inside the net.

Today, we had no interest in loaches and eels; we wanted fish – catfish especially.

We decided to start from the far end of our paddy fields, checking each corner until we reached the plunge mouth. When I say corners, I don't mean it in the usual sense of the word. Each paddy field had a discharge outlet, and whenever the water in a field overflowed, it went into the paddy field below through the discharge outlet. As time passed, a deep pond would form, and this was the so-called field corner. Some of these were large, and some were small; some were deeper than a man's height, while some would barely reach your navel. Fish and shrimps liked to stay in these ponds because the water was deeper than it was in the paddy fields.

To catch them inside the pond, we had to build a dam with mud near the outlet to separate the field from the pond. Then, we would stand inside the pond and bail the water out with our four basins. Very soon, the pond would be drained off, and the fish and shrimps could do nothing but struggle in the mud. Then, we put down our basins, caught them with a handheld net and put them into the fishing net.

After we had bailed a few ponds, we were a bit disappointed with our performance.

After having nearly broken our necks, all we had was tiny fish and shrimps. Usually, we loved to catch these because they tasted delicious after being roasted in a pan, baked dry in the sun and fried with some oil and salt. But this time, we only wanted catfish that were alive and kicking. We bailed for almost half a day but caught less than five of them, all small ones, about the size of a little finger, as if they had just been born the night before. They were no different from those tiny fish and shrimps. Sweating all over and covered with mud, we lay on the edge of the paddy field to take a break.

Everyone looked at me and asked: "Shall we continue?"

I said: "Of course! If not, what will the mother fox and her family eat for dinner tonight?"

Yisong said: "If we don't catch any large ones, let's take my family's big hen tonight."

Leping said: "No, we can't. We need to save chickens for the New Year."

Lemin said: "I think the ponds we bailed today are too small. A few dozen basins have drained them off. Think about it, how could large catfish hide here? We should find a refuge pond of a large paddy field, where the water is deep and rich in fish – big fish especially. You know, large refuge ponds have more weeds, and big fish like to hide there."

I was chewing on a blade of grass and thinking hard. My family didn't have many chickens. Where should we go to catch fish for the fox family? Lemin's words brought me to the realisation that playing in small ponds could only end in failure. We should go big! I spat out the grass in my mouth, propped myself up, looked at my defeated friends and said: "The biggest fish are hiding in large refuge ponds. Let's bail the largest one in our village – the refuge pond of Forty Paddy Field."

My friends all sat up when they heard this.

"Forty?"

"Forty? Can we handle it?"

"I'm afraid we won't finish until tomorrow!"

Forty was a paddy field near the plunge mouth, the largest one in our village. Its name had a very simple story. When our ancestors cultivated it and reaped rice for the first time, they harvested exactly forty *dan*, so our ancestors named it 'Field Forty'. No one knew when the word 'Field' was dropped, but 'Forty' was kept to this day.

In my eyes, Forty was so large that it seemed endless. The water in Forty was very deep, and, in my memory, it had never been drained, so a lot of fish and shrimps lived inside. My neighbour, Uncle Bufu, could make a fishing basket to catch fish. Once, he placed a small fishing basket at each of the four corners of Forty, and he was rewarded with a whole basin of catfish the next morning. He divided the fish between a few families, including mine. At Forty, even if you bailed the water out to catch fish there, you would still be able to harvest more catfish within ten days or so.

The refuge pond of Forty was so large that it might be more accurate to say that it was a small lake. Because Forty was located at the plunge mouth, whenever it rained heavily, the stream of water flowing down from the top layer of paddy fields would become stronger and stronger, and it plunged into Forty like a small river. Over the years, Forty's refuge pond got larger and larger. And it was very deep. I swam in it once, and the water reached my chest. We all knew there were lots of fish there, but none of us dared to bail it. Only the adults could do it because they had the strength and could use larger tools. That's why we all wanted to grow up quickly – the sooner, the better.

We hadn't yet grown up, so how could we dare to tackle Forty's refuge pond?

But after a lengthy discussion, we agreed that Forty was the only place where we would be sure to catch a decent amount of fish. After all, we needed to prepare enough food for the fox family to eat for at least a week, and we didn't have time to do this from Monday to Saturday because we had lessons.

Although we were not yet adults, we had grown up a bit since last year, hadn't we? We were stronger than last year, weren't we?

"Let's do it for the fox mother and her family. Let's bail the Forty!" Leping said. He was so anxious that he forgot to add the words 'refuge pond'.

Bailing the refuge pond of Forty was a totally insane idea, but we didn't have time to think about it.

Lemin said: "We can't complete our mission unless we bail the refuge pond of Forty."

Yisong said: "No time to waste! Let's bail! Even if we have to bail until it gets dark." He seemed to be much braver today.

We jumped up from the ground, packed up without saying anything and rushed to the plunge mouth.

When we arrived at Forty, we inspected the refuge pond and found it had been a long time since anyone had come to bail it for fish. We were overjoyed; there must be a lot of fish inside the pond. Catfish came up for air from time to time. From their barbels, we estimated that each of them would weigh no less than two Chinese ounces, and five of them would be one Chinese pound. How tempting it was!

On the side of the pond, facing the paddy field, was a long soil dam, which had been formed by flowing water over the years; it was very solid. There were a few breaches in the dam, but they were small ones, and we blocked them very quickly. The most difficult one to block was in the far west of the dam; over two metres long, it was the very passage through which the fish and shrimps swam from the paddy field to the pond. The wider the mouth, the deeper the pond would be and the easier it would be for fish and shrimps to swim into it. Therefore, to catch a good amount of fish, the outlet of the pond had to be wide.

We wanted to drain the pond to catch fish, so the first thing we had to do was block up the outlet completely. If we didn't do this, all our efforts would be wasted. We thought about the best way to do it, and we tried our hardest to bail the water out, but the water in the paddy field continued to flow into the pool. Were our efforts a waste? We would never complete the mission – not in a lifetime!

We started to build a dam for the refuge pond. That was indeed a chore. It took us quite a long time to build up the mud to stop the water in the paddy field from flowing into the pond. Everyone was aching all over in the end.

We were so famished that golden sparks danced before our eyes! We took out the cooked sweet potatoes from our baskets hurriedly. Within a minute, we had wolfed them down, and even the potato skins were swept away.

Draining off the pond was a continuous and repetitive task. Standing in the waist-deep pond, we four lined up and worked hard to bail the water out, basin after basin. After bailing for quite a long time, we looked back, and the water level had dropped only a little bit.

Yisong said: "My! Just that small amount after working for so long! When will we ever finish the work?"

I said: "A little bit is better than nothing. Let's keep moving forward."

Lemin and Leping put down their basins, stretched their bodies and rubbed their hands, saying: "No more complaints! Let's continue. We must drain it off!"

Splash!

Splash!

We held our basins and bailed the water again. Basins of water were poured into the paddy field. With our constant efforts, the water level was dropping millimetre by millimetre. But ten millimetres is one centimetre!

We were full of hope and kept bailing. Gradually, the pond became shallower, and the water level dropped faster – one centimetre, another centimetre. The water was level with our navels, then our backsides and then our thighs. The small fish and shrimps began to swim on the surface in a panic. We could hear the faint sound that fish made when they struggled to hide in water plants.

"I heard some catfish hiding in the holes!" Lemin shouted happily.

"Me too!" said Leping. "Seems like very big ones."

There were many small holes in the walls inside the refuge pond, very close to the paddy field above. They had been made by crabs. Some holes were big, and some were small, depending on their location in the mud. Holes above the water surface were often occupied by frogs, while those below the surface became the hiding places of catfish. The crabs loved to live in newly-built holes. They worked hard to dig a new hole, then abandoned it and made a new one, only to dump it again! In the refuge pond, they were unpaid architects, and the catfish liked them best.

At that moment, Yisong threw down his basin and, sounding as if he was about to burst into tears, shouted in panic: "We're done for! We're dead!"

We stopped to take a look. Good heavens! The dam had broken! There was a big crack in our newly-built dam, and the water from Forty broke loose and rushed without hesitation into the pool through the breach. Instantly, the pond water level rose. With no time to think, I dashed towards the crack and sat down on it with my back towards the paddy field. But the crack hadn't been blocked completely.

"Lemin, hurry up!" I shouted.

Recovering from his terror, Lemin ran to me and sat down beside me on the crack, stopping the mischievous water from Forty. Yisong didn't have time to cry either. He and Leping gritted their teeth, filled the basins with mud and dumped it behind Lemin and me to mend the breach.

When the water level on both sides of the dam was the same, the dam would stand there steadily, separating the paddy field and the refuge pond. But now that the water level of the pond had dropped, there was nothing to support the dam on one side, so the water pressure in the paddy field began to show its power. Our newly-built dam was made from soft mud, so how could it withstand the pressure from the water in the paddy field? How could the dam not break?

Seeing that Leping and Yisong had blocked the breach, Lemin and I stood up cautiously.

I turned it over in my mind. It wouldn't work. Our mud dam would probably break again. I said to my friends: "Let's add some steel bars to the dam!"

"Right! Add steel bars," they agreed.

We ran to the edge of the field, and each of us carried an armful of branches back. We stuck the branches deep into the dam, and it seemed to be more solid than before. We went on consolidating the dam for quite a while, making it stronger and thicker. Feeling more confident, we restarted our project of bailing the water.

The water level in the pond had already dropped to our ankles. We had to take a few steps back in order to continue bailing. We needed to work harder to pour the water out into Forty. By now, the water surface in the pond had been reduced by more than half, and the roots of the water plants were visible too. We spotted some speckled fish hiding in the grass; these fish didn't know they could hide in a hole, so they just hid in the grass or a small pile of sticks. Some of them went into the mud, but they couldn't stay there for long because they weren't clever enough; they had thought they were safe by hiding their heads inside the hole while leaving their bodies and tails outside. These speckled fish had markings that made them look like silver snakes, and that often scared people, especially when they tried to catch them. We left them alone for the time being. After all, they were like turtles in a jar, and there was nothing to worry about.

The water level dropped faster and faster, and we could see ripples stirred up by bigger fish as they scurried and fought against the water, while the small fish and shrimps were now struggling desperately.

We decided to start catching fish.

Before the speckled fish could swim back to the water and give us more trouble, we approached the water plants to catch one of them. I placed the net under its body and poked it with my finger, and it scurried into the net with a splash. We caught more of these hiding in the grass, searched the water plants thoroughly and caught a few more. We put them all into one basket, which was almost filled to the brim. We were so happy with the catch. The speckled fish, similar to catfish, could survive for quite a long time out of the water, but we still placed the fishing basket under the water; the basket had a lid, so there was no need to worry about these fish escaping.

Then, we began to pick up the small fish and shrimps struggling on the surface. Standing in the water, we collected them with our nets. The water became muddy, and more small fish and shrimps emerged from under the water. Very soon, our basins were full.

Next, our target was the other types of fish, including carp, crucian carp, dace, *nanei* fish and *lianglitiao*.

"Another one!"

"One more!"

Every time we caught a big fish, we shouted with excitement. The large plunge mouth was filled with our shouts and laughter. Wow, a full basket of fish! The first catch had already made us so satisfied.

It was still impossible to catch catfish though. While we were busy collecting speckled fish and the like, the catfish that were not hiding in the holes had already dived into the mud, playing dead. So we had to bail all of the water out.

The water surface got lower and lower, and very soon we had drained off the refuge pond. We started to collect fish for the second time.

We four stood in a row and dug the mud with both hands. Once we caught the catfish and loaches in the mud, we had to pull our hands back carefully because the catfish had poisonous external spines. If you should get stung, it hurt terribly, the wound would swell up, and it would take a few days to recover. We had learned how to bail the paddy fields when we were very young and had been stung by catfish many times, so we had accumulated some valuable experience. When we dug our hands into the mud, a slight touch would let us know whether it was a loach or a catfish. If it was a loach, we would hold it together with the mud, let it slide into the basin and then throw away the mud. If it was a catfish, we would open our fingers, explore the catfish slowly, seize it tightly by its head and lift it out of the mud. By this time, the furious catfish would be desperately shaking its two poisonous spines and making a scary crackling sound, but it was too late for it to make any attempt to escape, and it remained captive in our basket.

From the mud at the bottom of the refuge pond, we harvested a full catch of catfish, as well as half a basin of loaches, each of which was bright orange with two short barbells.

Finally, we cleaned out the holes – our favourite part. Each of us holding a long stick, we began to explore them.

When I was bailing the water, I had already fixed my eyes on the hole that these sly catfish had entered. I took the initiative and placed my net in front of the entrance. I poked the wooden stick into the hole and felt immediately that it had touched the soft body of a catfish. I poked it again, and a loud splash came through the hole.

Yisong was busy working beside me. When he heard the sound, he put his hand to his mouth and said enviously: "Wow, that's brilliant! Brother Jiang, there must be at least seven catfish in this hole."

I smiled and said with a nod: "This hole should rank first, shouldn't it?"

Lemin said: "I reckon I can find a hole with more catfish!"

Leping suddenly shouted: "Watch out! Snake!"

We looked over to the hole that Leping was poking and saw that a snake's head was coming out. It stared at us and flicked its pink tongue, sticking it out and pulling it in rapidly. It was very scary!

"Move aside!" I shouted.

We all kept back. Within a second, the snake darted out of the hole and plunged into the mud, splashing muddy water on us. It then shook its tail, climbed over the dam, leapt into the paddy field and wound its way forward. Watching it twisting away, we all stuck out our tongues.

Still frightened, Yisong said: "Could it have been a venomous snake?"

I said: "I can't tell. My dad said we must be wary of snakes whether they're venomous or not."

Yisong said: "My dad said that too. He said whenever we meet a snake, we should stay far, far away from it."

Leping was still poking the hole with his wooden stick.

Lemin smiled and said: "Leping, stop poking! There can't be any fish in a hole with snakes."

Leping said: "What if another snake is still hiding in it?"

I said: "We should be very careful, but snakes usually act alone in this season, so it's quite unlikely that there would be another one."

Still feeling worried, Leping checked the hole a few more times, and he didn't stop until he was satisfied there was nothing in there.

Next, it was my time in the spotlight. I said: "Now, look at me." I went on poking the hole I had found.

I moved the wooden stick a little bit, and a splashing sound came from inside. A catfish swam out of the hole slowly, and it entered my net obediently. I kept stirring the hole with the stick, and more catfish came out, one by one. Seven… eight… twelve altogether. They crowded inside the fishing basket, trying to hide under each other.

I poked the hole again. No more fish came out, though the sound of splashing could still be heard. The fish who still hid in the hole must be very smart – they knew they were sure to be caught if they went out of the hole. I had to use my hands to catch them. We all knew there would not be snakes in a hole with fish, so we could feel safe in doing this.

As I reached my hand inside, I discovered that the hole was very big and deep. To reach the very end of the hole, I had to press my chest against the entrance. What a huge hole! No wonder there were so many fish hiding inside. There were three left inside the hole, and they were bigger than the ones we had just caught. They were probably very clever. Showing no mercy, I invited them one by one into my basket.

After checking all the other holes, we again harvested a catch of fish – all catfish. Inside the basket, the catfish shook their fins, making a noisy, crackling sound.

We caught fish happily in the pond, totally unaware of how late it was. When we looked up after catching all of them, it was already dusk, and darkness was about to come.

We hurriedly jumped onto the field ridge. When we looked back, we found there was still one thing left undone. In our village, there was an unwritten rule that everything must be restored to its original appearance after bailing fish in a refuge pond. So we jumped into the paddy field again, removed all the 'steel bars' in the dam and put them ashore. Then, we bulldozed the dam and scraped away the mud to keep the passage free for the fish and shrimps. In this way, people who came to bail the pool in the future would be able to catch fish too.

The dam gone, the water from the paddy field rushed into the dry pond. The water level rose, little by little, and we stared at it in shock. It had taken us a whole day to dry it up, but now it filled up at once.

"Hurry up! It's getting dark!" I urged my friends.

We jumped onto the field ridge, carrying the heavy fishing baskets on our backs and holding the basins of fish and shrimps in our hands. We couldn't manage to take the nets as well, so we placed them beside the field for the time being. Walking down the rugged trail between the fields, we headed for our homes as the night grew darker and darker, talking excitedly, one by one, about what we had experienced that day.

A few torches shone ahead of us. Our fathers had come to meet us.

Four torches rested on us, and we stopped. Needless to say, they would see four boys covered all over with mud.

"I knew you boys must have gone to bail Forty!" my dad said. "You're very brave. Whether you've succeeded or failed, you're real men!"

I wanted to tell him we were sure to succeed. How could we fail? But I held back.

Uncle Bomin, Lemin's father, flashed a light on the basins we held and exclaimed happily: "Wow, you have quite a lot."

Yisong turned around and shrugged his shoulders in an attempt to shake the fishing basket tied around his waist. He said: "Well, those inside the basket count as well."

Our fathers marvelled as they tried to lift the fishing baskets on our backs. "They're really heavy! You boys are incredible!"

They took all the basins and fishing baskets, letting us walk without any burden. At that moment, I began to feel tired and hungry, almost unable to move my legs.

18
FAREWELL

We felt we had used up all our strength after bailing the pool for a whole day. It was the most tiring day we had ever had. I thought it might be even more tiring than making the round trip from home to school five times! We wanted to go straight to bed and sleep until dawn, but after supper we remembered we hadn't taken the food to the mother fox and her family. We had to hurry.

We decided to give them the other fish first – namely the carp and crucian carp. I shouldn't really call them merely 'the other fish' because, although most of them had died by the time we got home, they were still quite fresh. We thought we could keep the fish that were still alive and raise them at home for a period of time so that we could help the fox family a little longer. Besides, the carps and crucian carps had scales, and the mother fox probably liked eating fish with scales. Once they tried the fish with scales and found them delicious, they would probably accept catfish without scales when we took them later.

We put the fish inside a wooden basin, placed it quietly at the bottom of the pit and went back home, feeling relieved. It was my idea to use a wooden basin. I was worried that the foxes might not like plastic or metal ones. As they walked through the woods the whole night, they must feel familiar with wooden ones. I sacrificed my favourite wooden basin for them. When I placed the basin in the pit, there was a strong smell of foxes, and I felt assured that they were safe.

We took fresh fish to the mother fox for the next few nights, and the foxes happily accepted them and ate them up.

It was on the morning of the tenth day that we saw those two green lights again on our way to school.

"It's the mother fox!" sharp-eyed Lemin shouted.

"Yes, it's her!" I was overjoyed by what I saw.

As before, she looked at us for a while, then turned around and walked briskly along the mountain ridge towards the woods beside the Bachi River.

"She walks very gracefully – not limping anymore," Yisong said.

I was so happy for her. "She must have recovered and can find food herself."

"We are her friends now, so why did she still run in the opposite direction to cheat us?" asked Yisong with confusion.

"It's probably instinct," I said. "What's more, she might not recognise us."

"The five baby foxes must have grown bigger. Playing with them should be much more fun than playing with Blacky," Yisong said, full of yearning.

On our way back home after school, we decided to visit the home of the mother fox. There seemed nothing different, and the sun shone on the bottom of the pit, which was silvery and silent. But we immediately discovered that the catfish we had placed in the wooden basin were still there, untouched.

The mother fox and her family hadn't enjoyed the 'meal' we had given them the day before.

We hurriedly climbed down to the bottom to check. Yes, the fish were still there – all of them. We left some water inside the basin. These hardy catfish were still alive, and if you touched them, they would still make an angry noise, rattling inside the basin.

The silence made us very apprehensive. The special smell of foxes was gone.

"The mother fox has moved away," Yisong said, with great regret.

"It seems she moved away the day before yesterday; they left after eating the fish we gave them," Lemin said.

I agreed with him. If she had been there the previous night, the fish we had left earlier would not have been there. I said sadly: "It's a pity we didn't take a careful look last night when we left fish for them. And neither did any of us pay attention to whether there was still a fox smell,".

"I went down to give them the fish last night, and I remember I did smell their odour," Leping said.

"That's because it takes time for the smell to dissipate," Lemin explained. "Now, after two days, it's completely gone."

We collected the basin and the fish and climbed out of the pit. As the sun was setting, the surrounding mountains, the winding Bachi River and the terraces that stretched out to the riverside were all covered in mist.

Mother Fox, where did your family move to? Why didn't you tell us about it?

"Oh, I see!" I suddenly understood. "This morning, the mother fox was not going home – she came to say goodbye to us. It was as if she felt it hard to tear herself away from us. She didn't return to her previous home at all!"

"I think you're right," Lemin said. "Since she has a new home, she won't go back to her previous one for sure. If she had gone back to her old home, the fish we left for her wouldn't have been there."

Yisong said anxiously: "I'm worried about the five baby foxes. Will the trip to their new home be a long one? Could they keep up with their mother?"

Anyway, we didn't need to take food to the mother fox and her family that night. We hoped we could see them again one day. We knew we probably wouldn't recognise those baby foxes because they would grow into beautiful big foxes very soon.

Thinking of this, we all felt very happy though a bit lost at the same time. Whenever I looked at The Immortal Watching the Moon from Genma Ridge, and at the bushes in the navel of the immortal, I would think of the mother fox and her babies. They had once built their home there. I would say to myself: Mother Fox, if you meet any difficulties that you feel are too hard to overcome, remember to tell us. We'll help you again.

19
A SURPRISING REWARD

Teacher Ma announced in class that a recitation contest for seniors would be held. We had only one fifth-year class and one sixth-year class in our school, and there was going to be a contest between these two classes. We were all looking forward to it greatly.

Teacher Ma said there were too many students in the two classes, and it was impossible for everyone to take part in the contest. In our class, three boys and three girls would be chosen from those who signed up to take part. These six students would then represent our class in the contest. The contestants would recite an ancient poem, while a panel of judges, consisting of seven teachers, would score them. After excluding the highest and lowest of the seven scores, they would average out the remaining ones and get the final score for each individual contestant. Fifth-year students would have an additional one-point bonus. In the end, they would add up the scores of all the contestants for each class, and the class that got the highest score would be the winner. Teacher Ma told us that some TV contests used this scoring method and it was very fair. We did not have electricity, and we didn't know anything about TV, so we could only imagine what Teacher Ma was talking about, though even he himself did not watch TV with his own eyes. We felt this scoring method was pretty interesting though.

Would we four, who used to read *koutou* as *goutou*, be brave enough to sign up for the contest? It was a recitation contest, after all.

After having worked hard for a period of time, we were no longer the same students who first transferred to Tuanlong School.

Apart from overcoming Chinese Pinyin by mastering the consonants that we couldn't read or pronounce correctly, we also went out of our way to consult the Xinhua dictionary distributed by our school. It was indeed very difficult for us to read each character correctly and memorise each word, which equated to a babbling baby learning to speak. At first, we were more like a blind bear picking corn – picking one and dropping one.

Dad laughed after listening to our story. He said: "You boys should not regard it as a chore and force yourselves to do it. You need to fall in love with these characters, and then you'll be interested in memorising them. Our motherland is a large place with many ethnic groups. Without a unified language, things won't work at all. Mandarin is the standard Chinese language of our country. Our generation hasn't learned it well, but there's no reason for you boys to struggle with it. Remember, as long as you love it, you'll memorise anything that you want. If not, you won't be able to do it, even if it's simple."

This really was the case. The more we learned, the more we liked it; the more we liked it, the faster and longer we could memorise those characters. In the end, we all seemed to have a photographic memory.

The happiest time was when my dad bought us a transistor radio, the same size as a dictionary, specifically so that we could learn to pronounce characters in the standard way. He told us the Central People's Broadcasting Station broadcast programmes in the most standard Mandarin, so we could learn from them. In the programme *Little Trumpet*, we found the stories Grandpa Sun Jingxiu told were both interesting and easy to learn. This was broadcast from eight to eight-thirty in the evening, the time we studied together in my home. We listened to the stories every night, and we made great progress with learning Mandarin.

After that, whenever we spoke Mandarin, our classmates would no longer laugh. Of course, we knew their laughter was kind, and they never thought of hurting us. Teacher Ma said we now spoke better Mandarin than the other students; we knew he was saying that to encourage us. In the classroom, we no longer bowed our heads when a question was given to us; we dared to offer answers now.

Lemin, Yisong and I all decided to sign up for the contest, but Leping was a bit reluctant. He said: "I don't have any confidence. You guys try this time, and I'll think about it next time."

Yisong said immediately: "How long are you going to wait? Chances slip away without waiting for you!"

Leping replied: "I really can't this time. I know my limits."

I partly agreed with Leping. It's better to slow down when you're not sure enough. As for a contest, you should not force yourself to take part.

It took one lesson to choose three names from the list of candidates. All those who had signed up for the contest recited the same Tang poem, and the result shocked everyone. Two of us three from Najie Village won the chance to stand for our class: Lemin and me. When Teacher Ma read our names, our classmates all looked at us with admiration. Yisong failed to qualify this time, and I guessed it was because he was nervous and his recitation was not fluent enough. The third boy student on the list was Zhang Jianhong, while the girl students standing for our class were Li Xiuping, Lü Linying and Wu Xiaoyan. I suddenly thought of Cuiyun at that time; if she were still in Tuanlong School, I believe she would probably have made it onto the list because of her perseverance.

Teacher Ma must have seen the amazement and curiosity in all of the students' eyes. He walked towards me and said: "Huang Mingjiang, can I borrow your Xinhua dictionary for a second?"

I didn't know why he was asking for it, but I handed him my dictionary anyway.

Teacher Ma returned to the platform and addressed us. "You have all listened to their recitations, and the six students we have chosen are indeed the best in our class. You must be wondering how Huang Mingjiang and Wei Tianmin from Najie Village could make such rapid progress. Look at this!" He held up the dictionary and continued. "This is Huang Mingjiang's dictionary, completely dog-eared. Think about how hard he has tried and how much progress he has made! Boys and girls, you may not know this, but your classmates from Najie Village have to walk on the mountain road back and forth for about twenty *li* every day. What's more, they have made full use of this trip to study. Constant grinding can turn an iron rod into a needle! Today, it's inevitable that Huang Mingjiang and Wei Tianmin would stand out in the contest."

I heard the warm applause of my classmates.

In the end, our class lost the recitation contest. We did try our best, but even though we had six points bonus, the sixth-year students had been learning for one more year than us, and their final scores were still higher than ours. We accepted our defeat. To our surprise, an individual award was added after the contest, and I was given a prize for my personal high scores. The second prize went to a sixth-year student, Zhang Yechao.

How could there be an individual award? I came to know the reason after I heard the closing speech given by Principal Yang. Our school had just received a notice from the Baodong Township Education Group that a senior year elementary school recitation contest would be held in the town and each school would assign two contestants to take part. There were eighteen elementary schools in Baodong County, which meant there would be thirty-six contestants in total.

To be honest, I felt a little uneasy about suddenly being named as one of the thirty-six contestants. Or maybe it was fear. Was I qualified for this? I was representing neither myself nor Najie Village but our Tuanlong School.

Principal Yang called me to his office and said: "Huang Mingjiang, congratulations on winning the first prize in this recitation contest. I recognised your ability when you came here, and it's amazing that you could make such progress in such a short period of time."

I said: "Principal, even a blind chicken sometimes finds its corn. My winning this time is only a stroke of luck, and I know I'm not that good. You know, we've practised reciting this poem on our way to school, and we're very familiar with it."

I was telling the truth. In the contest, the poem given to me and my sixth-year opponent, Zhang Xiangjia, was *The Willow* by He Zhizhang, which we had indeed recited and discussed on our way to and from school. We really liked this poem, and when we recited it, we even tried to draw it with our fingers. So during the contest, I had nothing to worry about, and it just came out of my mouth naturally.

"Oh, a blind chicken finds its corn?" Principal Yang laughed. "I do hope we could have more such blind chickens! Practice makes perfect. Chance only favours the prepared mind."

I felt I had used an improper metaphor and smiled, embarrassed.

"You and Zhang Yechao will go to the county to take part in the contest on behalf of our school. What's your plan?"

I hadn't thought about this yet. "Principal, I really don't know what I should do."

Principal Yang said: "Huang Mingjiang, take it easy. Just do yourself justice in the contest. There's no need for you or our school to worry about your ranking or a prize. Just regard this contest as a routine classroom exercise."

On our way back home, all my friends cheered for my first prize.

"Brother Jiang, you've wiped out our disgrace. I'm so happy!" Leping exclaimed. His joy was beyond words.

I knew Leping was still obsessed with the laughter I had received when I was reading the text in class, but I didn't know how to respond to him.

Lemin said: "Brother Jiang, I do hope that you'll get the first prize again when you take part in the contest in Baodong."

Yisong said: "Brother Jiang will get it."

Leping said: "I'll be so happy if Brother Jiang gets the first prize again."

I was anxious and said: "I'm worried about it. Though Principal Yang told me to take it easy, disregard the rankings and think of the contest as a class exercise, I'm still worried. It's possible that I'll suffer a thorough defeat in the contest."

Lemin said: "Our principal was right. Think about the contest that was just held in our school. I was too eager to do well, and my result was not satisfactory. If I had recited the poem in a more natural manner, the way we used to do on the mountain road, like Brother Jiang, the result would have been better. Brother Jiang, I take back what I just said to you. It's fine as long as you do yourself justice in the contest."

Yisong added: "I still hope Brother Jiang wins first place."

The contest was held in the playground of Baodong Elementary School on a Sunday. All senior years of all elementary schools came – about five or six hundred students in total. It happened to be Baodong's market day, and a lot of people who had come to visit the market stood around the students; many of them were the students' parents. I saw my parents in the crowd too. In the student group, I saw my classmates from Tuanlong School, including Lemin, Leping and Yisong, led by Principal Yang.

I could see them clearly because I was sitting with the other contestants on the makeshift stage, above which hung a big banner with yellow letters on a red background: *Baodong Township Senior Primary School Students Recitation Contest*

Many colourful flags hung on the stage and were fluttering in the air. I saw a microphone for the first time, and there was a loudspeaker too. Hearing the wonderful music from the big speaker, I felt everything was fresh and interesting. In our school, we only had a very small speaker, powered by batteries. When the principal or a teacher needed to use it, they had to carry it on their shoulder and talk through it as they walked around.

What was even more novel was the contest format, which I had never seen before, nor even imagined. It surprised not only us student contestants but also the principals and lead teachers. It was not until half an hour before the contest that the format was announced: all the contestants were going to recite Chairman Mao's *Snow in the Pattern of Qinyuanchun.*

As soon as this was announced, all the contestants were separated from their classmates and teachers and gathered in a classroom to listen to a short lecture given by Teacher He Guanghua, the best and most experienced Chinese teacher in Baodong Elementary School. First, Teacher He read the poem twice, explained its content and background, highlighted characters we might read incorrectly, and then asked us to read after him. Finally, he said to us: "Remember to bow to the audience first when you're on the stage. Then introduce yourself like, 'I am so and so from such and such school. I am now going to recite *Snow in the Pattern of Qinyuanchun* by Chairman Mao.' After you finish your recitation, remember to say, 'That is my recitation. Thank you.' Then, bow again and go back to your seat. Students, is that clear?"

We all replied at the same time: "Yes!"

Teacher He said: "Good, now come with me, all of you!"

We all went up on the stage, where chairs had already been arranged. A note with the contestant's name was placed on each of the chairs. We found our seats quickly and sat down, waiting quietly for the beginning of the contest.

We all took out the poem and made final preparations.

After the contest, our principal and teachers all said they had never seen such a contest before, and they were really shocked. Even if they had wanted to give us some tutoring, they couldn't. It was indeed a contest where students had only themselves to rely on – a test of their improvisation skills, their adaptability, comprehension ability and accumulated knowledge. There was not even the chance for Zhang Yechao and me to talk to each other because our seats were far apart.

To be honest, on such a big occasion, although I was a little nervous, I just felt it was a new and interesting experience. Neither was I panicked by this kind of arrangement because I had never participated in anything like it before, and I thought it was just the way these contests were held.

I read *Snow in the Pattern of Qinyuanchun* silently first, feeling there would be no problem for me to read it aloud correctly. What I needed to consider was passion – Teacher Ma often told me that. He said recitation should be cadenced and rich in feeling so that the audience would feel as if they were there.

> *See what the northern countries show:*
> *Hundreds of leagues ice-bound go;*
> *Thousands of leagues flies snow.*
> *Behold! Within and without the Great Wall,*
> *The boundless land is clad in white,*
> *And up and down the Yellow River,*
> *All the endless waves are lost to sight.*
> *Mountains like silver serpents dancing,*
> *Highlands like waxy elephants advancing,*
> *All try to match the sky in height.*

The farthest place I had ever been to was Baodong, so how could I know what the north of our motherland looked like? I had never seen ice or snow, so how could I understand and appreciate the magnificent scenery of snow-covered land and frozen rivers?

At that moment, I thought of the shoulders of Mahuai, the Genma Ridge of Leimao Mountain. On one side of Genma Ridge was the mountain, while the other side was a cliff that dropped to the Bachi River. In the afternoon, after school, standing on Genma Ridge, you would have a feeling of pride when the wind blew from the river. Under the slanting sunset, Jia'ang Mountain, Longtang Mountain, Meihuai Mountain, Laiyou Mountain, Sanmiao Mountain and Lion Mountain stood upright into the vast and boundless sky, while the Bachi River wound its way along the bottom and disappeared into the horizon. In my eyes, the picturesque river and ridge were very much like the magnificent northern area depicted in Chairman Mao's poem.

I read it silently, trying to feel its artistic conception. Very soon, I had learned this grand and spectacular poem by heart, and I would just glance at it in case I might forget – you know, to be on the safe side.

The order of our recitation was settled by drawing lots. I was the twelfth one. After the contest began, I paid little attention to what was happening on the stage; instead, I was lost in reading the poem silently. I didn't stand up until the host read my name. Standing in the middle of the stage, I looked at the crowd and saw the row of our Tuanlong School and my parents standing right at the back of the crowd. I calmed down gradually.

I made a low bow to everyone, walked over to the microphone and said: "I am Huang Mingjiang from Tuanlong Elementary School. Today, I will recite the poem *Snow in the Pattern of Qinyuanchun* by Chairman Mao." Applause burst out from below the stage.

I cleared my throat. In front of me, it was no longer the audience who was listening to me. I felt as if I were standing on Genma Ridge, and next to me were my friends, Lemin, Leping and Yisong. What I was facing right now was the magnificent mountains and rivers in my home town. A surge of passion ran through me. I began to recite the poem:

> *See what the northern countries show:*
> *Hundreds of leagues ice-bound go;*
> *Thousands of leagues flies snow...*

One line after the other, I hardly looked at the draft in my hand. My heart swelled with lofty spirit and pride as I recited this magnificent poem. When I got to the part 'Brilliant heroes are those / Whom we will see today', I seemed to see Mahuai running back and forth, carrying mountains on his shoulders, followed by the people of our Najie Village and my friends too.

I ended with the words: "That's my recitation. Thank you." I heard a shower of warm applause bursting out onto the stage. It was then that I was drawn back from Genma Ridge. I lowered my head with embarrassment and went back to my seat.

The results were announced. I got 97.30 points, the highest score, and I won first place! In second place was a girl named Zhou Yanfang from Baodong Elementary School. Zhang Yechao scored 93.80 points and came fifth in the contest. The judges commented that I was "smooth and fluent, rich in feelings and accurate in pronunciation".

When the teacher presenting the awards handed me the certificate of accomplishment and a glass trophy of a little man who was kneeling and reading a book, he stroked my head and asked me secretly: "Great job! Had you already learned it by heart?"

I said: "No, I hadn't. It's my first time to recite this poem. To be honest, *The Red Army Fears No Hardship of Expedition* is the one I'm familiar with."

When we went back to the Tuanlong School group, my teachers and classmates all applauded me and Zhang Yechao for our performances. Principal Yang said: "Huang Mingjiang and Zhang Yechao won the contest using their own skills. Congratulations!"

I handed the certificate and the trophy to Principal Yang and said: "Headmaster, I want our school to keep this."

Principal Yang smiled and took them. He told me these would be displayed in the honours room of our school, and I would get a copy of my certificate.

The happiest time was when I went back to my parents. They just smiled and looked at me without saying anything. Then, all of a sudden, Dad put me on his shoulders and carried me across the street, regardless of the fact that there were so many people around. I tried several times to get down from his shoulders but failed. He crossed the street and carried me down to the rice noodle shop where he bought each of us a bowl of freshly made rice noodles.

As we were eating, my mum put her rice noodles into our bowls and sang softly:

> *Le ah le luo,*
> *The calf just stood up,*
> *The singer just got on the stage.*
> *The road ahead is still far away.*
> *Mountains await to be climbed, and seas await to be crossed.*

I never forgot the taste of this bowl of freshly made rice noodles!

20

THE MOST IMPORTANT FESTIVAL

One day when I got back from school, I found my home was full of people, all wearing smiles on their faces. From the kitchen, the crisp and bright *liaoluo* of my mum and the other women floated out, and so did the fragrance of the meat boiling in the pot.

The moment I entered the gate, I saw my grandmother busy setting the table and benches. I shouted: "Grandma!"

She put down her work and stroked my head affectionately. With a smile on her face, she said: "Lejiang, you're back! You've grown taller in a few days!"

Uncle Bofu, our neighbour, carried his bench to the table and said: "Grandma Jiang, your grandson is really amazing. He has won first place in the town!"

I blushed and asked Grandma: "Where is Grandpa?"

Grandma said: "He's chatting with friends in the living room!"

In the Zhuang language, *jiang'guo* means chatting, while *jiang'gu* means telling stories.

I ran into the living room and saw my grandfather was sitting there chatting with a few elderly men, all looking very joyous. I greeted him, put down my school bag and ran into the kitchen.

Singing *liaoluo* happily, Mum and her friends were picking up coils of long, red sausages from the big wok and then placing them into a big winnowing basket. The red sausage had already been cooked and gave off a tempting aroma. Mum and her friends picked up the sausages with chopsticks and, from time to time, used their hands to support them. The red sausages, fresh out of the wok, were very hot, so they couldn't hold them for long and let go of them very quickly, blowing and puffing, which interrupted their *liaoluo* quite often.

I asked: "Mum, it's not festival time, and it's far from the third of March. What on earth is the festival today?"

Mum did not answer. Instead, she cut a few slices of the red sausage from one end of the coil and gave them to the other women who were busy working. She said: "Sisters, try this to see whether it tastes good." Of course, she gave me one slice – a particularly thick cut.

I took a small bite and exclaimed at once: "Wow, it's so yummy!"

Mum said: "Silly boy. You don't have the final say."

The other aunts all said: "It tastes very good."

In our village, we loved to make red sausages whenever we killed pigs in a festival. Women soaked glutinous rice in advance, then mixed it with pork blood, together with seasonings like fennel seeds, sand ginger and star anise. The mixture would be used to fill sausage skins before being tied, coiled and cooked in the wok. They were removed from the wok to cool thoroughly, sliced and put into a big bowl. That was the beloved red sausage of our village. All of the red sausages were delicious, but the women's culinary skills often determined whether they were of the very highest quality. The red sausage my mum made was sure to be the most delicious of all.

I was reluctant to swallow the slice in one gulp, so I just tasted it little by little, enjoying the exceptional delicacy. Mum smiled, cut one more slice for me and said: "We're celebrating a festival that we've never had before. It's bigger than the New Year Festival and much bigger than the Double Third Festival! Lejiang, Land Distribution to Households has started in our village! Everyone is overwhelmed with joy, so we killed the pig we have raised together for the New Year celebration. All the villagers are here. This is indeed a big, happy event, a rare occurrence for us."

The 'Household Contract Responsibility System' was also called 'Distribution to Households and Farmers' Land Contracts'. People in our village liked to make things easy, so they just cut it short and named it 'Land

Distribution to Households', like they shortened 'Forty Paddy Field' to 'Forty'. It was said that this policy started in many places in the late 1970s, but because of our remote location it had been delayed in our village. As far as I knew, drylands on the mountain had long been secretly distributed to households in our village, and vegetable gardens had also been given to each household to take care of. That's why we were able to plant so many sweet potatoes and raise pigs for the New Year Festival together.

The extra slice of red sausage my mum gave to me was so precious that I could not bear to eat it myself; I wanted to share it with Lemin, Leping and Yisong. Mum laughed and said: "How could you boys share one slice of red sausage? Come and take more." As she said this, she cut three more thick slices and put them in my hand, saying: "Take these and keep the one you just got for yourself."

At this time, Dad and a few uncles came in, holding pots of pork and hog viscera. They usually killed the pig by the side of the river and carried it back to cook. They saw the delicious red sausage slices in my hand.

Wearing a shy but bold smile, Dad said: "This red sausage looks so good. Could we try a slice too?"

"No way!" Mum pretended to put on a straight face. "You have to wait until dinner time!"

Laughter burst out among the aunts. They started to discuss it noisily.

"Try some? You are men!"

"If you want to try some in advance, change yourself into us women, who cook with spatulas!"

"Or change into children!"

"Then, it's easier to wear long hair!"

"Ha ha ha!"

Hearing the laughter of my mum and the other aunts, Dad and his friends began salivating. Pretending to be upset, Dad said: "We'd better not become women – otherwise, who will plough the distributed land!"

My mum stopped laughing and said: "That's right. We all rely on your hard work. Come over here!"

She cut a few slices quickly and fed these, slice by slice, into the mouths of my dad and his friends, saying: "You greedy men! This is our reward for you. Do your farming work well after eating this slice of red sausage!"

Laughter burst out again in the kitchen.

I no longer paid attention to the adults and rushed out to look for my friends.

Lemin and the others had also heard the news about the pigs being killed, and they ran to look for me the moment they put down their school bags.

Under the big banyan tree at the edge of our village, we sat on the intertwined tree roots and enjoyed the delicious red sausage I had brought with me, talking about the main event that all the adults in the village had been discussing. We had no idea how important this event was, but we knew that as long as the adults were happy, the whole village would be happy, and we would be happy too.

I said: "I've never seen those adults as happy as this!"

Yisong said: "Yes, happier than the day they were threshing rice on the threshing floor, everyone beaming cheerfully!"

Leping said: "If only they could be so happy every day! Then I wouldn't have to be scolded so often by my dad."

We all knew Leping's dad, Uncle Boping, had a hot temper and liked to wear a long face, especially when things didn't go well for him. Leping was sure to suffer if he was not careful. So I said my dad was the best. Hearing that, Leping thought about it for a while and said his dad was good too – he had a heart of gold.

With a subtle expression on his face, Lemin whispered: "Good news! It's indeed sheer luck that Forty Paddy Field has been distributed to our four families! Of course, there are some other fields as well. I heard it averages out at three *mu* of land per person."

"Really?" We were pleasantly surprised at the news and jumped from the tree roots.

Lemin said: "I just heard it on the road here from Uncle Bopeng. He said to the other people that lots were drawn, and Forty was distributed to Bojiang, Bosong, Bomin and Boping. Isn't that our four families?"

"Let's go and have a look," I said to my friends. We immediately headed for the big plunge mouth and arrived at the paddy field.

Beside the Bachi River, Forty was as wide as usual, sparkling with gold under the setting sun, nothing different from how it used to be. The refuge pond was still there, and fish still made noises when they swam to the surface to take a breath. But now we knew Forty was different. It had become the rice field of our four families and was going to be taken care of by us from now on. The more we looked at it, the closer we felt it was to us.

When we ran back to the village, people were all seated – men and women, young and old. Each household had brought a pot of fragrant rice. Elders were invited to sit around large, ancient square tables in the hall, and the other adults sat in the courtyard. We children did not occupy much space, which saved tables and benches. On the flat ground outside the gate, there were two bamboo mats that were used for bathing corns. We sat in two circles on the mats; we all liked to eat like this because it was more free and comfortable. If you sat with the adults, you had to behave. Well, we could do that when we grew up.

Because it was not the New Year Festival or the Double Third Festival, adults did not need to prepare ten or twelve dishes to worship our ancestors. We had two dishes today: red sausage and a huge pot of pork, pork ribs and hog viscera cooked together. Mum and the other aunts ground a lot of tofu. They cut the tofu into big cubes, the size of a fist, fried them in the peanut oil until they became pale yellow gold, and then cooked them with the pork in the pot. The pork bones were placed into another huge pot and stewed with eight or ten pounds of rice until they became delicious porridge that was available to anyone who wanted to have a bowl of it.

I liked red sausage and pork soup, especially the tofu cooked with the pork, which tasted tender and fresh and yummy. Seeing that we ate so fast, Mum added another big scoop for us. She said: "Boys, eat more but don't stuff your bellies so full or they'll burst!"

The adults ate meat, and they drank soup and wine. They talked about the future farming, the harvest and anything else they could dream about. Then, they began to sing *liaoluo* and *jiate*, as if they were willing to exhaust themselves even when they were eating the food.

We didn't review our lessons that night, and we didn't have a lot of homework either. The main reason we weren't doing any work was that we had to give our bamboo-shoot lamp to the elders. They ate and drank less, but they talked a lot. I went to bed early while they were still chatting, and I had no doubt they would talk until dawn.

21
A REPLY

It made sense to stand high and see far ahead. As we became more and more accustomed to the new lessons of the fifth year, and as we worked harder and harder to bone up on the old texts, it was easier for us to understand the parts we used to find difficult. Besides, we had made up our minds to study every day, leaving no single question unanswered. We insisted on working wholeheartedly to make everything clear until we thoroughly understood.

It's true that heaped-up earth becomes a mountain!

The ten-*li* journey to school had become more and more enjoyable. We four, as one, made progress.

Since I was the eldest and also the leader of the group, I set a higher standard for myself: I should be able to help Lemin, Leping and Yisong with their studies as our teacher did.

I had reason to do this. When we reviewed homework at night, our teacher was not able to come from Tuanlong and help us; we could only wait until the next day when we were at school, which was indeed very time-consuming.

The best way was for me to help solve all the problems like a teacher would do, leaving no questions overnight.

To do this, I had to understand everything clearly during class time. I finally worked out a method, namely consolidating pre-class preparation. Every night, after Lemin and my other friends left my home, I would sit alone under the bamboo-shoot lamp and spend extra time learning in advance the new text that would be taught the following day. In this way, I would know which parts I could handle and which I could not. When I was in the classroom the next day, I would listen to the teacher attentively. I needed to make sure that I truly understood the parts I felt I had already mastered, and know the reasons why I could not understand the other parts. Gradually, and quite unnoticed, I learned how to study by myself, and my expressive skills improved greatly as well. When we studied together at night, I began to help my friends with their problems, and I could do it quite clearly and knowledgeably.

Yisong said: "Brother Jiang, you're our teacher now."

I said: "Far from it! Let's keep working harder."

In the second periodical test, we not only passed but scored above seventy points! I scored eighty-seven in Chinese and eighty-five in maths. In fact, if we had not been affected by the first periodical test and had not been so nervous, we would have scored even higher.

At the meeting for reviewing the test, our class teacher, Mr Ma, praised us and said: "In this test, the students from Najie Village have made great progress. Their perseverance in study is worth emulating by the whole class. Though their performance is not the best in our class, they have made huge progress compared with the results they had in the first periodical test."

All eyes in the classroom were on us. I felt my face burning, and I was very embarrassed.

Teacher Ma continued: "Now I want to invite Huang Mingjiang to talk about how they made such good progress."

Without any preparation, I stood up amid the applause and intent looks of my classmates, totally at a loss and not knowing what to say. I just stood there, rubbing my sweaty hands.

Teacher Ma smiled and encouraged me: "Mingjiang, what about saying something about how your study group works together and how you have tried to catch up. Don't be nervous. The audience members in front of you are your classmates who are studying with you every day."

I tried to calm down, but I just couldn't do it because I had never thought I would be standing before my classmates to introduce our study experience. I summoned up all my courage and tried to say something. Though I didn't speak Chouqing Mandarin anymore, I stuttered. I said: "We don't have any experience, and we just want to catch up with all of you. So we decided to 'mend holes' and study so that we could grasp all the lessons we had not fully understood in the past. We just went over everything we needed to cover as we walked on our ten-*li* journey to and fro every day."

Did I still have something else I wanted to say? I just couldn't think of anything, so I had to finish my talk by saying: "That's all. Thank you." Then, I sat down.

The warm applause in the classroom made me very uneasy. Teacher Ma took the lead and continued to explain what our 'mend holes' meant. I couldn't hear a word because my head was spinning and buzzing like a beehive in chaos.

On our way back home after school, we didn't review our lessons as usual. We felt excited because our efforts and progress had been approved and appreciated by our teacher. Everyone said our efforts were worthwhile, and we would continue to work harder to learn better.

Tasting the joy of victory, we were so pleased that we skipped and jumped all the way home. As we talked with each other, the topic moved to my speech in the class.

Yisong said: "It's the first time I've seen Brother Jiang so shy – his face was as red as a cooked crab! Ha ha!"

Lemin said: "Honestly, Brother Jiang's speech in the class was a bit... erm... It was weird. Why did he begin to stammer when giving a speech while he is so talkative with us? Brother Jiang's speech won't get a pass, will it?"

Leping said: "Brother Jiang, when you were speaking in class, I did want to help you out!"

Yisong asked immediately: "Brother Ping, what was your plan to help Brother Jiang?"

Leping said: "I don't know. If it was about building a dam or bailing water to catch fish, I could do more to help. Seriously, what can I do to help Brother Jiang?"

Listening to my friends, I was speechless, feeling my face burning again.

"Think about it – Brother Jiang managed to finish what he wanted to say after all. If I had been asked to do this, I would not have been able to say that much!" said Lemin.

Leping added: "After all, we didn't mean to show off when we planned this, did we?"

Yisong said: "Let's pass Brother Jiang's speech, shall we?"

"Pass! Pass!" they shouted together.

Could such an awkward speech be passed? It must be a joke! But…

Yisong asked me with a smile: "Brother Jiang, what do you think? Does it deserve a pass?"

I said: "Wait a second. I agree with Leping. We didn't do this to show off, but I really did a poor speech. How could it be passed? I think we should 'mend the hole' here as usual."

We happened to be at Genma Ridge, so we sat down on the rocks. I took out a piece of paper and a pen, spread the paper on my knees and said: "Now, let's rewrite the speech."

Leping said: "We need an address first – 'Teacher Ma and all my classmates…' or something like that."

Lemin said: "We need to be modest first. Modesty helps one go forward. You know, something like 'We actually don't have any experience to share…'"

Yisong interrupted him and said: "Brother Jiang mentioned this already."

The discussion went on with everyone joining in, and I came up with this:

Dear Teacher Ma and all my classmates,

As students from Najie Village, we did make a little progress in our studies, but it is far from enough, and there is still a big gap between the other students in our class and us. We need to work harder and make further progress to catch up with them. We really don't have any experience. We want to get more help from the teacher and our classmates, and we will be very grateful for that.

When everyone read it, they all said it was better than what I had said in class.

A REPLY

Yisong, however, shouted: "But there's no sharing of any experience at all!"

Lemin said: "We don't really have any experience, do we?"

That's exactly what I wanted to say. When I thought of my attempt to stammer out some so-called experience in the classroom, I felt very embarrassed.

"OK, that's what we four students from Najie Village want to say."

I stood up and said: "Let's read it aloud one by one. Let's read it to Leimao Mountain and the Bachi River."

From Genma Ridge halfway up Leimao Mountain flew our 'verse' and our 'chorus'. This was our small but firm promise to the mountains and rivers in our hometown.

On our way back, I suddenly thought of Cuiyun and the letter that she had written to us. We had not replied to her yet. I said: "We should write a letter to Cuiyun."

"Goodness, how could I forget about Cuiyun?" said Leping, patting his head.

Yisong said: "Yes, let's write a letter to her. I have so many things to tell her."

"What should we write?" I asked them.

Leping said: "Let's read Cuiyun's letter again and answer everything that she asked."

Yisong laughed: "Brother Ping, are you doing an 'Answer the following questions' exercise?"

Leping smiled sheepishly.

"Let's write about our study first."

"Don't forget the mother fox."

"Let's tell her that Brother Jiang won first place in the county primary school students' recitation contest."

"How about the two tests?"

"Are they included in the study part?"

"And the harvest of the black olives."

"Exactly, the black olives we bring for lunch – they all taste yummy."

"And those crispy and delicious fried small fish and shrimps!"

"Bailing fish in Forty Paddy Field should be included in the letter."

There were so many things that we wanted to tell Cuiyun. We couldn't stop talking as we walked on the mountain road.

In the evening, I wrote a letter to Cuiyun:

Cuiyun, our dear classmate and sister,

Hello there! We have long received your letter, and we are sorry not to reply to you until today. Please forgive us.

As usual, we go to school before dawn. We recite new texts on our way to school because we want to catch up with our classmates. We don't want to waste any time, you know. We keep on studying together every night like we used to do together. We have reviewed all the old texts and thoroughly revised everything we learned in the past. We have made progress gradually. In the first periodical test, we all failed. Our names ranked first, second, third and fourth on the list in our class – of course, from the bottom of the list! That was indeed humiliating, and we didn't want to tell you this. But we didn't lose heart. In the second periodical test that we have just had, we managed to catch up with our classmates a little, and Teacher Ma praised us and asked us to share our study experience. You know, we don't really have any experience. It is simply the truth that clumsy birds have to start flying early. We have to grind our teeth to move forward, and we have the confidence to catch up and surpass our classmates.

Cuiyun, is everything all right with you at your new school?

We met a mother fox at The Immortal Watching the Moon. She had five cute cubs. The mother fox was wounded later, and we managed to saved her. But she moved away, and we don't know where she and her babies have gone.

I almost forgot to tell you one thing. We had a big harvest of black olives that my second great-uncle had planted for us. There was lots and lots of fruit, and each family had a share. The whole village had the fragrance of cooked olives. We have them for our lunch, and the fish and shrimps we caught in the refuge pond were delicious too. You would definitely love our lunches. Cuiyun, they would taste more flavourful if you were here eating with us.

We haven't had any heavy rain and the Bachi River has not risen a lot. Sometimes it rises a little bit. Land Distribution to Households has started in our village, and I heard your grandmother has a share too. That is all for now...

We wish you good health and big progress in your studies!

From Qin Hanping, Wei Tianmin, Huang Mingjiang and Li Yisong

I didn't mention winning first place in the Baodong County reading contest for primary school students. It was, after all, an individual award, which was not something big in my mind. I felt embarrassed to put it in the letter anyway.

22
FATHER'S BIG FISH TRAP

Everyone was present in the evening class tonight, and our fathers were there too. We reviewed our lessons and did our homework while our fathers discussed how to manage Forty Paddy Field. We read our texts aloud and discussed our questions while they whispered and talked with each other in low voices.

But our loud voices were no match for their whispers. After we finished our homework, we ran to them, listening to their discussion and then joining in.

Leping asked first: "How will we divide Forty into four parts? Shall we build field ridges to do that?"

The adults looked at each other with knowing smiles.

Leping's dad, Uncle Boping, said: "Are we dividing gold?"

Yisong said: "Divide Forty with a cross through the middle? Won't it take a great effort?"

Lemin said: "Field ridges will take up a lot of land too. It's not worth our while, is it?"

Dad said: "We've discussed it already. The policy of Land Distribution to Households will remain unchanged for at least thirty years, and you boys should take part in it as well. You know, the land will be given to you when you grow up, and you'll manage it when we're old. Here's our plan. The paddy field resembles a chessboard, almost the same length on each side. We've decided to nail a wooden stake in the middle of each side. When you look to the opposite side from the stake, Forty will be divided into four parts. As for which household gets which part, let's draw lots. Each household can plant the field section separately. Besides planting rice, we can do some business cooperatively in this field, in our leisure time. What do you think about this?"

I said: "Won't it resemble the Chinese character for 'field'?"

"Exactly!" All the adults agreed.

"How will we run a business together?" asked Lemin.

"We're discussing this right now," said Uncle Bomin. "We plan to introduce fingerlings into the paddy field, and there'll be an income when the transplanting season comes the following year. We can also introduce some grass carp to get rid of the weeds."

Yisong said happily: "Then Forty will turn into a big pond where fish are sure to grow fast."

Uncle Bosong said: "If we succeed, we'll have fish soup to drink next spring."

We were yearning for fish soup.

Once our fathers made a decision, they would carry it out immediately. On market day in Baodong, they collected some money and sailed four small boats to the market to buy fingerlings. They bought a lot of toe-sized carp and placed them into Forty. When we were on our way home after school, we saw the field ridge of Forty had been strengthened. A few bamboo poles tied with some straw thatches were stuck inside the paddy field. These told people that there were fingerlings inside the field and no one should trouble them, and neither should fish be bailed there. Of course, it was OK if someone came to place a small fish trap in the refuge pond of Forty to catch catfish. If our carp should swim into the fish trap, those who placed the trap would be sure to put it back into the field. There was no need to worry about that.

My dad had another idea. He planned to catch some big carp in the river and put them into the refuge pond. When spring came, they would lay eggs and breed. One way to catch big carp alive was to find a spot and place bait there. When the carp gathered to eat the bait, it was time to cast the net and catch them, but this would usually take too much time and effort. Another way was to place a big fish trap in the river – usually at the plunge mouth –

through which the water in the rice field would flow into the river. Carp looking for food would swim into the fish trap involuntarily. You just needed to keep checking it, which would not take much effort.

Putting big fish traps in the river was not difficult, but making them was by no means an easy task, and even if you were able to make one, you were not guaranteed to catch fish. Fish loved to swim into the big trap my dad made, which was quite well-known in our village. When he was asked the reason why less fish would swim into traps other people made, my dad would explain that the slope of the trap opening was the key issue. If the opening was too flat or too slanted, the fish would turn back and swim away when it touched it with its head. Only when the slope of the trap opening was sufficient would the fish be willing to enter. My dad didn't know how to explain the method for making a proper trap opening – he just looked at it and continued his work if he felt it was OK; if not, he would dismantle it and start again. I think he relied on his experience and feelings, which indeed was really difficult for others to replicate.

Dad cut down a few bamboos and spent two days completing four large fish traps. He put some bait, such as fried peanut bran, into the traps and placed them at the four plunge mouths.

The next morning when he went to check the traps, he came back empty-handed. He said the new traps smelt strong and the fish were still on the alert. This needed patience.

The following day was Sunday. Dad asked my friends and me to go and check the fish traps.

When we arrived at the Wangpa Ferry, the sun had already risen to the height of the bamboo tops. We had planned to get up early and asked our parents to wake us, but none of them did, as if they had already made an agreement with each other.

We each had a chopper tied to our waist. We had made a decision that, after we checked the fish traps, we would search in the woods beside the river for some hardwood. We wanted to make a few spinning tops and have a good battle with each other for a whole day! The harder the wood, the better it would be, because the spinning tops made of hardwood were more steady, and they could withstand the force when they bump into each other, sometimes knocking their opponents off. Besides, they make an extraordinarily loud sound when spinning – quite powerful. No one wanted to lose in today's battle!

Many boats were moored at the ferry, and we eventually chose the one belonging to Leping's family. Their boat was brand new, so there was no risk of leakage. It sailed so swiftly that it seemed as if it would jump out of the water. Sitting in the boat, people looked more energetic. My family's old boat leaked everywhere, and we had to fix it with red earth, mending holes here and there. When sailing it in the river, you had to bail water out with a bowl all the way. Uncle Boping had already agreed to let us use his boat today because there was no work to do on the other side of the river.

Leping was familiar with his boat, and he also said he was the strongest among us, so he did the rowing. Standing at the stern, he backed the boat out, adjusted the bow and set off. We decided to check the fish traps upstream, one by one, starting from the Meitian plunge mouth. The boat glided briskly on the surface of the river. The morning mist was slowly dissipating, and the sun was reflected in the river, laying a piece of silver-white silk in front of us. Sitting behind Leping, Yisong put his hand into the river, letting the water flow through his fingers, which made a very pleasant sound.

Lemin and I stood at the bow of the boat. As Leping rowed, the boat charged forward in the water, and our bodies followed its rhythm; it was very comfortable.

Lemin scared Yisong by saying: "Yisong, don't you know there's *sanzhualang* in the river? Your hand is perfect for them to bite off and swallow in one gulp!"

Yisong hurriedly took his hand out of the water. Then, he saw Lemin smiling and realised he had been fooled. He said: "You're kidding me! *Sanzhualang* live in Genlong Pool – they can't be here." As he said this, he put his hand into the river again.

Lemin said: "Can't they swim here from Genlong Pool?"

Hearing this, Yisong took his hand back out again quickly as he stared at the bottomless river in panic.

Sanzhualang, a huge, softshell turtle, would occasionally poke its head from the water for some fresh air. We met one once in Genlong Pool when we went to look for rose apples along the riverside the previous summer. It looked black, and its shell resembled a huge pot. It saw us too and sank down slowly.

We were so frightened that none of us dared to make any sound for fear that it might turn our boat over from under the water. We didn't dare to pick the crispy rose apples along the riverside and fled from Genlong Pool in panic.

"Stop frightening him! Let's talk about whether we'll find anything in the first fish trap!" I said.

Yisong said: "If there are any fish, they'll be small ones at most."

Leping stopped rowing and let the boat coast along. He said: "We might find some, but it's also possible that we'll leave empty-handed."

Lemin teased: "Leping, what you just said is meaningless, isn't it?"

Leping started rowing again and replied: "OK, so you tell us whether we can or not."

Lemin said: "I'm not sure about it either."

Leping laughed. "Is there any difference between your words and mine? Brother Jiang, we want to hear what you think."

Honestly, I wasn't sure about it either. I said: "Let's hope today will be different."

The fish trap was tied up by two huge green vines attached to a water poplar tree that spread over the river. Leping rowed the boat towards it. Standing at the bow, I grabbed one green vine, while Yisong, at the stern, grabbed the other. We pulled the vines together to drag the fish trap out of the water. At the very beginning, there was no sound at all. Yisong sighed and said: "It's empty!" But before he even finished his words, I heard some clicking coming from the vines, the sound that fish made as they knocked their heads on the fish trap. The fish inside the trap were alarmed by the noise and tried to escape.

"Fish!" Yisong and I shouted at the same time. We speeded up, and the fish trap was quickly dragged to the surface of the water towards our boat. There were two fish thrashing and splashing inside the trap.

"Two carp!" We could see clearly that two golden carp had jumped in the trap, and we hurriedly pulled it onto the boat. The trap my dad made was so huge that it almost filled the cabin of the boat. The tail part of the trap faced the bow, and the opening was just in front of us. But my dad had placed the stopper on the opening very tight for fear that the fish might knock it open. It took Lemin and me a lot of effort to open it.

We lifted the trap up and poured the two carp, which weighed about one Chinese pound each, into a small, enclosed tank located close to the bow of the boat. The tank had two or three small holes drilled in the bottom, and these were usually plugged with stoppers. When fish were put into the tank, the stoppers would be unplugged to let the water in through the holes. This meant that the water inside the tank was the same as the water in the river, and the fish would live for a long time.

We reset the opening of the fish trap and placed it back in the river carefully. Our first victory! We were all indescribably happy.

"There are indeed fish in the trap! I was right, wasn't I?" Leping said.

Lemin said: "If you got the right answer, we four did too."

I said: "Regardless, we have caught fish!"

Yisong said: "If each trap should catch two fish, four traps means eight fish. If each fish is as big as the ones we just caught, that will amount to more than ten pounds."

I said: "Right. And if each of them lays one thousand eggs, that will be about eight thousand!"

Lemin asked me: "Are they all female fish? The smaller one we just caught seems to be a male one."

I turned it over and discovered that he was right. But even if half of them were male fish, the other half would each lay one thousand eggs after they were put into Forty Paddy Field, which meant thousands of fingerlings next year!

We discussed it enthusiastically. Leping kept the oars in his hands and rowed towards the big plunge mouth.

At this time, four small bamboo rafts clattered from downstream. Snow-white fishing nets hung on each of them, and a row of ospreys was perched at their front. We knew they must be the fishermen who worked along the Bachi River. Each raft was made of three large bamboo poles with their exteriors scraped off, and these were tied closely together. The two ends of the rafts tilted up and moved swiftly. On each raft stood a man holding a bamboo pole in his hands. When they forcefully pushed the poles deep into the river, the rafts whistled forward – much faster than our boat. They silently passed us and headed for the big plunge mouth upstream. We knew they wanted to arrive there earlier than us to catch the fish.

Suddenly, I thought of what my dad had repeatedly warned me: if someone came to fish with ospreys, we must tell them to avoid the river section where we had placed the fish traps. Otherwise, if the ospreys should enter the fish traps, they would not be able to get out, which would be a great loss to the fishermen.

Honestly, what people in our village hated most were those fishermen who came here from other places. When we went fishing, we usually built a fishing spot with bait first and then cast nets, or we attracted groups of fish together and threw the net later. But these fishermen were different. When they came, not only did they take away a lot of fish but the terrible smell of their ospreys would scare away the fish that we had painstakingly attracted to the fishing spot. It was indeed the most irritating thing. Once the fishing spot became useless, it would take quite a long time to become functional again. But to be fair, the Bachi River belonged to everyone, and there was no reason for us to forbid them to fish there. What's more, they didn't have any paddy field to plant and only made a living catching fish. We understood them.

I shouted to them eagerly: "Uncles, stop for a minute. Please stop!"

They looked at us blankly, paying no attention at all. Their bamboo poles pushed deep into the water, and their rafts continued to rush forward. We four therefore shouted together, and they stopped their rafts at last.

We approached them. Their rafts were lined up in a row, and they were staring at us with cold and watchful eyes. They remained silent.

I said: "Uncles, don't fish in the huge plunge mouth ahead. There are…"

Before I could finish my words, a relatively young man pointed forward and asked: "You mean that big river inlet ahead?"

"Yes."

"Why?" he asked.

"We have placed big fish traps there! It's very dangerous," Yisong said.

They exchanged looks and sneered.

"Fish traps? In that river inlet ahead?"

"Yes, exactly!" Leping said. "Our fathers told us that we must remember to warn people who come to fish here with ospreys in case something bad should happen."

"Ha ha ha!" They burst out laughing in delight.

We looked at them suspiciously, not understanding why they could still be so happy after they knew the danger.

A white-haired man with a moustache said: "Boys, your parents told you to say that, didn't they?"

"Yes, they told us," we said. Was there any doubt about it?

"Well, let me tell you. We've heard too much of it," a younger man said. "Boys, stop trying to trick us like your mums and dads."

I was anxious upon hearing this. "Uncles, we're not tricking you. We did place fish traps there."

They just wouldn't listen to us. They pushed their bamboo poles into the river, and the four rafts were off towards the big plunge mouth like arrows. I guessed they must have come to fish here more than once and knew this section of the river very well.

Lemin said angrily: "Huh! Let's wait and see. They are sure to suffer. A good man's sayings are seldom untrue!"

Lemin was surprised too and said: "Aren't they asking for trouble?"

Yisong just felt confused: "We kindly reminded them, but they said we were tricking them. What's more, they criticised our parents. It's so ungrateful of them. I've never seen such shameless people!"

We were upset and felt very uncomfortable. Leping slowed down his rowing. When we arrived at the big plunge pool, those fishermen had already prepared the gill net and started rocking their bamboo rafts up and down to drive their ospreys into the river.

It was the first time we had seen fishermen using ospreys to catch fish. It was indeed an extraordinarily noisy scene. Those men pushed their bamboo poles and rocked their rafts constantly. The rafts rose and fell and patted the water, making loud splashing noises. They kept shouting at those lazy ospreys that had flown back to the rafts, driving them to the river with their bamboo poles. They also called back the ospreys that had caught fish and carried them in their mouths. When ospreys catch fish, they usually try desperately to swallow them; unfortunately, each of these birds had a ring around its neck, which made it impossible to swallow anything big. The fishermen would take the fish from their mouths unmercifully and throw them into their fish basket. The ospreys would get some rewards though –their masters would pick up small fish from a basket behind their backs and throw it into their mouths. Then, the ospreys were driven back to the water again.

"Look, a big fish!" Yisong shouted.

Two ospreys came up from the water with a very big carp caught in their mouths, and they swam towards the bamboo raft.

Yisong was quite envious. "Wow, what if my little Blacky could catch fish like that! If we had ospreys, it would be much easier for us to catch fish."

Lemin said: "I heard that fish caught by ospreys don't live long."

I said: "Look, their fish baskets are just placed on the bamboo rafts. Indeed, those fish could not live long."

At that time, the men stopped rocking their bamboo rafts and shouted to their ospreys: "Come back, come back."

Very soon, the ospreys came back to their masters' rafts. They quacked very noisily as they shook off the water from their bodies and wings.

At this time, however, the relatively younger man, who had said we were liars, was yelling as hard as he could. "Jiabao, come back! Jiagui, come back!" His anxious and impatient shout had already taken on a tearful tone.

"Oh no!" I immediately knew something had gone wrong. Shocked, I said: "Leping, row the boat to check the fish trap, immediately."

Leping also felt something was wrong. He quickly brought the boat about and headed for the big plunge mouth. He had inexhaustible strength. Our boat shot forward, throwing up splashes at the bow.

The fishermen stared blankly at us as we sailed past their bamboo rafts. Our boat rushed straight forward and banged against the shore. Lemin and I lost our balance and fell into the river.

We hurriedly vaulted onto our boat, grabbed the thick green vine and pulled it out of the water with all our strength. Yisong stood at the stern and grabbed the other vine, trying to pull it out with Leping.

When the fish trap was close to the surface, we found two struggling things inside it. We knew it had to be the ospreys.

"Hurry up!"

"Hurry up!"

The fish trap was dragged onto the boat, and inside it were two ospreys struggling with their eyes rolled back. The fishermen came to their senses at last, and the four bamboo rafts came over to us quickly.

Lemin and I tried desperately to open the fish trap, hoping to release the ospreys as soon as we could. But Dad had fastened the trap so tight that we failed, even after exerting all of our strength. I felt for the sheath around my waist. There was no time for me to think about it, so I hurriedly pulled out the machete, slashed at the trap and ripped it open wider with my hands. Working together, we set the trap upright, and the ospreys fell from the big opening onto the bow.

With the ospreys, three golden carp fell out as well. They flopped and leapt about on the boat and then jumped into the river in the blink of an eye, leaving nothing but a train of water bubbles.

"Our big carp!" Yisong almost cried with anxiety.

"Alas!" We all uttered a long sigh as we stared at the foam left by the carp.

The bamboo raft of the younger fisherman had already stopped beside our boat. He held up the two ospreys that were still struggling and thanked us again and again.

Yisong said angrily with tears: "We told you clearly in advance, but you just wouldn't listen. Now our fish trap is broken and we've lost our carp."

The four bamboo rafts stopped around us. The fishermen looked at the broken fish trap and the glistening fish scales left by the carp.

One grey-haired fisherman said: "We must compensate these boys."

The uncle who got his ospreys back said: "It's on me. Boys, please take this basket of fish."

I shook my head.

The grey-haired fisherman said: "One basket of fish is not enough. Please take all four baskets."

I said: "It's good enough that nothing happened to your ospreys. The fish that your ospreys have caught can't live much longer." I waved my hand and said to Leping: "Let's go back home first. Lemin and I need to change clothes, and I'm feeling cold now."

Bringing the broken fish trap with us, we rowed the boat away, leaving the fishermen standing on their bamboo rafts, shocked and speechless.

Before our boat went far, we turned our heads and shouted towards them: "Uncles, please remember, we have also placed fish traps in the two river inlets ahead."

I thought that this time they would believe us, wouldn't they?

23

A SUDDEN BLOW

Dad said I had done the right thing when he heard about this. He said a new fish trap could be made if the old one was broken, and carp could be caught again if they got away, but the death of an osprey would deprive the fishermen of their bread and butter. Ospreys were fishermen's treasure to make a living, and they could not afford to lose them.

I asked Dad whether we could mend the broken fish trap. After all, it would be a waste to throw it away.

Dad said: "Silly Lejiang! The fish trap stinks after the ospreys have been in it, and it's very difficult to get rid of the smell. Fish have sensitive noses, so they won't swim into this trap again. Throw it away. I'll make a new one at once."

Little by little, our fish traps caught eleven golden carp in total. We placed them all into the refuge pond of Forty, hoping they would have a lot of children and grandchildren. We put three signs in the refuge pond, similar to the ones we put in Forty. Dad said we didn't really need to do this because people knew there were fish inside the paddy field and they wouldn't come to bail fish in the refuge pond.

Big fish were unwilling to swim into traps that were either too new or too old. When fish traps had been soaked in the water for a long time, they would become covered with a layer of mud and turn blacker and darker, so it would be very difficult to catch fish with it. These would become a hiding place for *juchan* fish, catfish and *guding* fish, which were small enough to swim through the holes in the traps. If anything alarmed them, they would escape immediately through the holes, and there was nothing we could do about it. If we wanted to catch them, we had to use small fish traps with tiny holes, but the river fish did not like these; they preferred to hide in 'high-rise buildings'. So, after a period of time, the four big fish traps in the river had completed their historical mission and were retired, honourably. Dad was worried that fishermen might still come to fish here with their ospreys, and those traps would cause trouble again, so he fished them out of the river, dragged them to the shore and destroyed them.

I had never seen the people in my village being so diligent. They were busy working on their contracted land, preparing for the next year's harvest.

My dad was trying to establish an orchard. He had long taken a fancy to a place named Carp Head, which faced the south and had fertile land. He wanted to plant lychee trees there. He was very fond of a variety called *jizai* lychee in Guangdong. I tried some once. With thick meat and a tiny seed in the middle, this kind of lychee tastes sour and sweet – very delicious. Moreover, its fruit are uniform in size and look adorable – a light, elegant colour. Dad decided to introduce *jizai* lychee and build a production base. If he succeeded in doing this, he would be able to help the villagers to plant lychee. Dad told me that Second Great-Uncle was addicted to planting fruit trees because he wanted everyone in our village to have fresh fruit to eat all year round and to make the whole village rich. After the implementation of the Household Contract Responsibility System, Dad's idea received strong support from village and township leaders. He had already started to clear the site.

It was during this time that the people in our village discovered that a lot of places in our country had practised Land Distribution to Households since the end of 1978. In such a remote area, our village was behind by quite a few years. No one in our village made any complaint, and they all said: "As long as our country practices reform and opening-up, it's a good thing. It's not a big deal to be behind for a while. Isn't it often said that he who laughs last laughs longest?" If the adults were happy, then we would be happy too.

But then, my happiness disappeared.

One day, when I came back from school, I saw my grandmother helping to prepare food to feed our pigs; this was indeed very rare. Mum seldom bothered Grandpa and Grandma for fear that they might get tired helping with the housework.

I asked: "Grandma, what are you doing here?"

Grandma looked very sad and said: "Something has happened to your mother."

I was terrified by her words. "Grandma, tell me, what happened to Mum?"

Grandma told me the whole thing. Mum and Dad had gone to work in the orchard. Grandpa had been suffering badly with rheumatism, so my mum took the chance to look for some herbs for him. As her attention was on the herbs in the grass, she failed to watch her feet and accidentally stepped on a wasps' nest hidden in a hole underground. It was after the ninth of September in the lunar calendar, and wasps were busy raising the last batch of their young – the largest batch. During this time, wasp attacks were particularly aggressive, and wasps that built their homes in holes underground were the most ferocious type. Alarmed, the wasps flew out of their hole, surrounded my mum like a huge black cloud and then stung her like crazy. Mum had to flee as quickly as she could. Unfortunately, it was a slippery place with rocks and slopes, and she fell down the cliff to the ground below. She did escape the wasp attack, but she knocked herself against a rock and broke her right leg.

Dad put Mum on his back and rushed to the ferry. Uncle Bofu and Aunt Meifu happened to be there, and they helped them get to the health centre in Baodong.

"Mum!" I couldn't help bursting into tears, thinking that she must have suffered a lot.

Grandma said: "Your mum is now in hospital, and nobody knows when she'll be back. I'll stay here with you for a few days."

"Grandma, did you see her? Is she hurt badly?"

"No, I didn't. Your dad carried her all the way from the mountain to Wangpa Ferry, but when he went back to get some money, he asked me to tell you that there was nothing seriously wrong with your mother and you should not let it affect your studies!"

How could it not affect my studies? It was quite impossible. When my friends and I reviewed our homework that night, I was restless, as if my soul had left my body. All I thought about was my mum, and I could not concentrate at all.

It happened so suddenly that none of my friends knew about it, and neither did I want to let them know, so I just kept it a secret.

Lemin sensed that something was strange. He asked: "Brother Jiang, what's the matter with you tonight? It's so unusual for you to make a mistake on such a simple question."

Yisong said: "Yes, Brother Jiang is like a dreamer tonight."

Hearing that, I could not hold back my tears and said: "My mum was injured, and now she's in hospital."

"Good heavens!" All my friends jumped up in shock.

Yisong said: "No wonder I didn't hear her tonight. I had a feeling that something was missing."

I said: "I just want to see my mum."

"Let's go to Baodong now. We have experience of walking at night, don't we?" Leping said.

My friends eagerly packed up their school bags. As the captain of our study group, I calmed down a bit and said: "I can't bring trouble to you – it will affect your studies. None of you should go. I'll go to Baodong myself. If I can't get to school on time tomorrow, please ask Teacher Ma to grant me leave. You can help me make up for the lessons tomorrow night."

But my friends were still worried, and they didn't want me to go to the hospital alone.

I thought about it and said: "How about this – let Leping come with me while Lemin and Yisong go to school tomorrow as usual."

Lemin said: "Good idea. We'll ask our parents to prepare more food for tomorrow, and we four will share."

Grandma, who had heard our discussion, hurriedly came over and said: "You boys are not going to Baodong at night. Uncle Bojiang warned against this many times. You must not go. Please don't make your parents worry about you. Walking such a long way at night will just cause worry. What's more, even if you were there, you boys wouldn't be able to help much. Lejiang, I know you're missing your mum, but please don't make her worry about you – she will get better sooner that way. Be a good boy!"

Thinking that Grandma was right, I finally gave up on the idea of going to Baodong.

I tossed and turned in bed, thinking about my mum and unable to fall asleep for a long time. When I woke up, my dad had already cooked the food, but there was no sweet *liaoluo* from Mum. It felt like the sky had fallen.

"Dad, any news of Mum?"

"Don't worry. Your mum is feeling much better. The hospital applied some antidote for the wasp stings. And the best news is that her broken bone has been aligned and put into splints. It will be restored to its rightful position soon. She can come home in a few days after observations. Aunt Meifu is taking care of her, and everything is going well. Stop worrying about your mum and concentrate on your studies, will you?"

Dad had got back home in the middle of the night.

On our way to school, I told my friends about my mum's situation, and they felt relieved. We decided to locate the exact spot where my mum had been stung by the wasps, so we could avenge her by setting fire to the wasps' nest.

I was absent-minded during class. I had never been like this before. I just saw the teacher's lips move but could not concentrate on what he was saying. I really couldn't listen at all. After the first class, I went to see Teacher Ma to ask for a leave of absence. I said: "Teacher Ma, my mum was injured, and she's in hospital now. I want to ask for permission to go and see her at the health centre in Baodong."

Mr Ma was very concerned about my mum's situation. After he asked some details, he said: "Huang Mingjiang, it's good of you to bear the pain of your parents in your mind. It's the responsibility of a man. Go and see your mother. Please send her my regards and wish her a quick recovery." He quickly wrote down 'approved' on my leave-of-absence note, and he signed his name too.

I immediately packed up my school bag, informed Lemin and my other friends, and rushed out of school.

Sweating heavily, I arrived at the Baodong health centre. At the door of the ward, I saw Aunt Meifu. She was very surprised to see that I had arrived so early.

I asked her anxiously: "Aunt, where is my mum?"

She said: "The doctor is seeing your mother inside."

My mum's weak voice came from the room: "Is my Lejiang here?"

A man's voice was next. "So soon from Najie Village? You have a good son. Come on in." I guessed that this was the doctor.

I dashed into the ward, and the doctor said to me: "Your mum is very brave. The splint has been placed on her leg, and it has successfully held the broken bone in place. We have done the X-ray, and the bone is in the right position now. Boy, don't worry. We'll also apply some traditional Chinese medicine. She's expected to recover in a month or so. Now that you're here to visit her, she'll get better even sooner." Then, he left the ward.

It was at this time that I saw my mum clearly. She was lying in bed, her face swollen like a pumpkin because of the wasp stings. The swelling reduced her beautiful big eyes to two thin lines, and she could not even open them. She laid motionless on the bed, her right leg stretched out.

"Mum!" I cried, tears running down my face like a river bursting its banks. I buried my head in her arms.

"My good Lejiang!" Mum softly stroked my head and my cheeks. She also had tears rolling down her face.

"Mum!" I wiped her tears with my sleeve.

"Lejiang…" I knew my mum wanted to smile at me, but she just couldn't, which I totally understood. My friends and I once got stung by bees when we ventured to take honey from some honeycombs. Our faces quickly swelled up and became numb. Our heads got extraordinarily heavy, and it felt as if we had hung a stone around our necks.

"Lejiang, who cooked for you this morning?" asked Mum. Her voice sounded very weak.

"Dad."

"So he slept very little last night, did he?"

"Yes, it was very late when Dad came back home. I don't even remember the exact time."

"Did he sing a *jiate* when he woke you up?"

"No."

"Your dad is unhappy."

"Mum, I only like to hear you sing *liaoluo*. I'm sad when I don't hear your *liaoluo* in the morning."

Mum was speaking with great effort because of her swollen face. "Lejiang, sunny days can't last forever, and our lives are full of ups and downs. It's inevitable that we will encounter troubles and disasters, but sunny days are sure to come after the rain. During hard times, we should never let our heads go down like wilted bean sprouts. Do you agree?"

I nodded my head.

But after a while, my mum sighed: "Well, Land Distribution to Households has just started in our village. Your dad and I are trying to plant our field well and make good preparations for our lychee orchard. But my leg is broken. This is indeed bad timing. People in the village are busy working while I have to lie here. What bad luck!"

"Mum, stop thinking like this. The doctor said you'll get better soon. Don't worry, Dad and I will take care of our family."

Mum said: "It takes a hundred days for bones and muscles to recover. This has kept me from my work. What's more, I don't know how much money it will cost."

I said: "Mum, as long as you recover, the money will be well spent. Don't worry, have a good rest. You have Dad and me. There's no difficulty that we can't overcome!"

Mum said nothing but heaved a little sigh. From her swollen eyes, a few crystal teardrops rolled down her face.

I didn't know what to say, so I asked: "Mum, you haven't had your lunch, have you?"

Aunt Meifu, who was standing beside us, cut in. "Your mother hasn't had anything since she came here yesterday. I brought her breakfast this morning, but she didn't eat."

Mum said: "I just don't want to eat anything."

"Mum, I've brought some lunch with me. Let's eat it together."

"Did you come all the way to see me without eating anything?"

"Dad made this lunch for me. It's delicious. I don't want to eat it on my own. You haven't tried it before. You must have a taste."

I took the spoon Aunt Meifu had bought and put a mouthful of rice to her lips. Mum opened her mouth with difficulty, took the food and chewed slowly. I tore a small piece of olive fruit and put it into my mum's mouth.

"Mum, is it good?"

"It's delicious."

"Everyone says the olive fruits that you made are the most delicious!"

"Lejiang, you must be hungry too. Come and eat."

"OK. I will."

Although I was hungry, I wanted to save all the food for my mum. I knew she would only have a better appetite when I was with her. Slowly, I fed her the meal and occasionally took a small mouthful for myself. Dad had fried some pork with the black olive fruits, and I saved all of this for my mum.

Aunt Meifu said: "Lejiang, what a blessing that your mum has such a good son as you."

Mum said: "This is the best meal I've ever had in my life!"

"Mum, let's do it again tomorrow. I want to have lunch with you like this."

Hearing that, Mum was anxious. She said: "No! No! I can't affect your studies. I'm very happy that you came to see me today, but just this time. No more! Your Aunt Meifu is here taking care of me. You and your dad don't need to worry about it."

24
LOVE

Lemin, Leping and Yisong asked about my mum every day, and they all wanted to visit her in Baodong. I told them my mum wouldn't even allow me to go again, let alone them.

By Saturday, I couldn't wait any longer. As soon as school was over, I grabbed my bag and rushed to Baodong.

"Brother Jiang, wait for us!"

Before I had got far, I heard the shouts of my friends. It didn't take long before they caught up with me.

"Brother Jiang, we must go to see your mum today whether she allows it or not!" said Lemin.

Seized by a nice warm feeling inside, I said: "OK. Let's go!"

Upon arriving at the health centre, we rushed into the ward together. I was overjoyed by what I saw and shouted excitedly: "Mum!"

The swelling on my mum's face had gone down. She had resumed her lovely and elegant appearance. She leaned back on the bed, slowly moving her ankles and exercising muscles as directed by her doctor. When she saw us, a smile appeared on her face.

"Hey! You all came here!"

Everyone was happy when they saw my mum looked so well. They said eagerly: "Hello Aunt! We wish you a quick recovery. We always feel we've lost something each night when we review homework in your house without you."

Mum stroked their heads, one by one, and said: "Thank you all for coming to see me."

"Mum, I'm so happy that your face is not swollen!"

Mum said: "How could the swelling not go down when all of you care so much about me? The Lord is unwilling to let you boys see a face that's swollen like a big pumpkin."

We all laughed.

I said: "When I saw my mum's swollen face a few days ago, I hated those wasps."

Leping said: "Aunt, tell us where that wasps' nest is. We'll burn it."

Yisong continued: "Yes, send them all to hell. Let's take revenge for you."

"Never ever do that," said my mum, waving her hands. "In fact, it's my fault. Think about it. Wasps build their homes and make a living there, doing no harm to anyone. If I had been a bit more careful, I would have noticed them flying in and out of their nest, and I wouldn't have stepped on its entrance. Seeing someone threaten the safety of their children, how could they not fight back desperately? Indeed, if someone should dare to do harm to any of you, we, as mothers, would be sure to try our best to protect you without hesitation. No mercy for sure."

My mum's words did make sense, but we were still very indignant when we thought about what she had suffered after being stung by those wasps. We had long made the decision to burn this wasps' nest, so it was not easy for us to change our minds for the time being.

Mum looked at us and continued: "It was indeed my fault, not the wasps. What's more, it happens to be the dry season. You're young – what if the burning of the wasps' nest should lead to a mountain fire? That would be really horrible. Boys, you must listen to me. Don't bear the wasps a grudge, and don't set fire to this nest that brought me pain, will you?"

We still resented it anyway.

"If you boys don't give me a promise, I'll worry about it. Look at me." Mum smiled and pointed at her hair. "Now my hair is black, but if you insist on burning that nest of wasps, my hair will turn white immediately, and I'll become the white-haired woman in the drama."

We couldn't help but laugh at this.

"Sons, promise me you won't burn that wasps' nest."

"I promise," I said.

"Me too," Lemin, Leping and Yisong promised, one by one.

A boy should keep to his word. Though we still hated that nest of wasps, which had done so much harm to my mum, we dropped our idea because we had promised her to her face.

It was probably out of curiosity that, one day in the winter holiday, we finally found that wasps' nest. It was in a secret place with weeds covering its entrance, so difficult to notice that it was no wonder my mum had stepped on it.

But not a single wasp could be found inside the nest, leaving just an empty shell, like layers of stacked, dried cow dung. It had echoes of the poem *Yellow Crane Tower*: "Once gone, the yellow crane will never on earth alight."

That was how wasps lived. After the ninth of September in the lunar calendar, they bred their last batch of children for the year, abandoned their nest and flew away. Older and weaker wasps could not survive the harsh winter while some of the last batch hid under rot leaves or inside a tree hole. Those survivors, who struggled to make it through to the next spring, had a tenacious vitality. In the gentle spring breeze, they would build their new home. At first, their hive was as big as a spoon hanging upside down with only two or three children inside; then it grew to the size of a pear, and then a bowl, with more and more children and grandchildren, a strong army already. In less than half a year, the nest would be as big as a huge paddy basket, occupied by an army of thousands.

Of course, they would give up their nest once again before the arrival of the harsh winter and prepare for a comeback the next year. The way they struggled so ceaselessly and tenaciously was truly awe-inspiring.

After the doctor used a splint to fix my mum's injured leg, he applied some traditional Chinese herbal medicine externally to speed up the healing process. Mum recovered very soon. After a week, her leg was not painful anymore. Two weeks later, the doctor removed the splint and asked my dad to bring her home and take good care of her there. The doctor said we needed to continue with the external application. He also said that Mum could do some muscle recovery exercises. Four weeks later, she could walk a little with crutches. By the seventh week, she could basically go back to her normal life without crutches, although she couldn't carry anything heavy until her leg had completely recovered.

One day, when I got back home from school, I saw my mum sitting at the edge of the bed with no splint on her leg. I jumped for joy.

"Mum, you're back finally!"

Mum said: "I feel like I've been away from home for a few years!"

When Mum was at home, it was a rich, warm and high-spirited place. When she was not there, it was cold and empty.

I threw down my school bag and ran out at once. I just couldn't wait to tell Lemin, Leping and Yisong. When they heard the news, they looked even happier than me.

Having Mum around and hearing her voice at home, I felt particularly at ease and was full of strength when I was doing the housework. No matter what I did – chopping plant leaves for the pigs, cooking their meals or preparing dinner for my family – everything seemed to go smoothly.

As I held a bucket full of food at the pigsty, I heard banging on the door.

I put down the bucket and asked: "Who is it?"

There was no answer, but the knocking on the door continued.

I walked over to the door, opened it gently and looked out. It was a black dog. It jumped over the threshold and squatted in front of me, wagging its tail, staring at me happily and barking softly.

It was Yisong's Blacky!

Yisong, Lemin and Leping were rushing towards my home, sweating all over. Yisong said: "The moment I made a gesture, he ran directly to your home. I couldn't catch up with him. I was afraid he might run to the wrong place."

Leping held a porcelain basin in his hand. There were two or three pounds of fragrant honey inside. All three of my friends smiled shyly.

I understood at once. They must have gone to get some honey from the old longan tree next to Tunmeizhang, the fish pond. Fresh honey was only available there, but the nest of wild bees was ferocious. The whole village knew that, and seldom did anyone dare to ask for such trouble.

"You went to take honey from that nest of bees beside Tunmeizhang?" I asked them anxiously.

They grinned and nodded their heads.

"Let me check." I looked at their faces worriedly.

"No sting on my head, just a few on my body," Leping said casually.

Yisong, who used to be very timid and shy, said bravely: "I'm getting a bit addicted to being stung by the bees!"

"My right hand became their main target," said Lemin, "but I heard that bee stings can treat rheumatoid arthritis. If so, we won't get rheumatism in this life, will we?"

I checked closely and saw quite a lot of small red spots on their bodies, especially on their right hands and arms. I knew they must have taken turns to reach into the tree hole for the honey, which of course made them targets of those bee soldiers. Leping had strong muscles, and there were still four or five pulsating bee stings on his arm. It was agony for him as I pulled them out, one by one, and threw them away.

We all knew a bee could not get its sting back after it had attacked someone. These gallant bee soldiers, who bravely protected their home, would leave their bee colony and die slowly.

"Brother Min had a good idea," said Leping. "We pierced a few thick plastic bags with an awl to make them breathable. Then, we placed the bags over our heads and tied them tightly around our necks so that the bees couldn't get to our faces."

I had once experienced the fierceness of this nest of wild bees; it was very intimidating. Whenever I thought of the day I suffered that crushing defeat and ran away, a chill would run down my spine. Now, for my mum, my friends had run the gauntlet, and it was hard for me to express my gratitude.

Leping handed the honey they had gathered to my mum and said: "Aunt, this is the oldest and sweetest honey. You're sure to recover quickly after you eat it."

My mum's eyes turned red. After quite a long time, she said: "There's no other place in this world where we could find better boys than you!"

25
A TEMPORARY PLAN

I cooked the rice and fried the dishes, but Dad hadn't come back yet. I asked Mum to eat first while I waited for Dad.

Mum said: "It's been quite a long time since I last ate with you two. Let's wait for your dad together."

I untied the herbal medicine from my mum's injured leg and helped her soak her feet in hot water to improve her blood circulation. Then, I applied the new herbal medicine to her leg. Just as I had finished everything, I heard familiar footsteps outside.

"Dad's back!"

I went to greet him happily. He had an axe on his shoulder.

"Dad, good news – Mum's back."

"Oh, that's good news," said Dad, putting down his axe. "It should have been me who told you this."

"Did you already know about this, Dad?"

"Silly Lejiang, it was your dad who carried me on his back from Baodong," said Mum.

I was silly – how could I not have realised this?

After supper, Dad told us about his plan, and he wanted to know what Mum and I thought about it.

He said we didn't have any savings at home, so we had borrowed a lot of money for my mum's injured leg. No household in our village was well off, and the faster we could return the borrowed money, the better it would be. He planned to dig a kiln and make some charcoal with the wood that had been cut down when he was preparing the orchard.

Dad explained: "Winter is coming. At the Baodong Ferry, charcoals sell pretty well when winter comes. Drivers who go to Nanning or Beihai love to take some charcoal with them for the winter. We were going to sell the wood as firewood, but it would have taken until next year for it to dry completely. Also, we don't have enough hands to ship so much wood to Baodong. Firewood is really cheap, and it's difficult to sell too, so our efforts would be wasted. But if we fire a kiln of charcoal with the wood, we might be able to pay off the debt this winter. What's more, we might even have a little spare to buy good seeds, fertilisers and lychee seedlings."

Mum was very worried. "How can you do so many things by yourself? I'm unable to help you after all."

Dad said: "Don't worry. I'm a bull with inexhaustible strength. What's more, I did this before, and it's not a problem for me at all. The hillside behind the orchard is rich in thick and fertile red mud, which is a perfect place to set up a kiln. I've already started it today!"

"Dad, let me help you. Many hands make light, and better, work."

Dad was very happy. "Does that mean my Lejiang agrees with my idea? Lejiang, when we encounter difficulties, we have to figure out ways to solve them. There's always a way. Difficulties will never disappear by themselves. Never! We must remember this truth."

The next morning, I heard my mum's sweet *liaoluo* again, but it was still Dad who cooked the porridge and prepared lunch for me. Mum hadn't got over her leg injury, and Dad wouldn't allow her to do any housework.

Before I left home, I asked Dad: "Are you going to dig the charcoal kiln today?"

Dad said: "Yes, I'd better do it quickly and try to dig one as large as possible. I'm hoping that one kiln will produce a thousand pounds or so of charcoal."

"Dad, I want to do this with you!"

"It would be great to have a helper, but you're still young, and your task now is to study. Don't worry – go to school. I can manage by myself."

I arrived at school on time, but I couldn't concentrate on my studies. I forced myself to listen to class attentively, but I fell into absent-mindedness from time to time. After drifting through the four lessons in the morning, I finally worked out a method and went to look for Teacher Ma.

I told Teacher Ma that my dad had decided to make and sell charcoal to solve the current difficulties we faced. I explained that my dad had started digging a kiln, and I wanted to help him. During this special period of time, I promised to work as hard as I could in the morning, and I would leave to help my dad in the afternoon. As for the lessons I should miss, I would ask my friends to help me make up for it. In this way, I could help my dad and keep up with my studies at the same time.

"Teacher Ma, please approve my request!" I said.

Teacher Ma hesitated for quite a while and asked: "Is this what your dad asked you to do?"

"No, he didn't. He said I'm still young and my task is to study. He told me not to worry about things at home. But Teacher Ma, I'm a big boy now, not young anymore."

"Afternoon lessons are not the main consideration here. It's good that you understand the hardships of life from a young age." Teacher Ma hesitated, but he eventually agreed. "At most, it takes a few days to dig a charcoal kiln. I'll talk about it with the principal later."

When I went back to the classroom, Lemin, Leping and Yisong were waiting for me to have lunch. I said to them: "I'm going back home to help my dad dig the charcoal kiln. You must study hard in the afternoon and teach me everything you've learned in the evening."

I ran straight from school to where my dad was digging the kiln. He was already inside, and I could hear the thwacks of his shovel hitting the dirt.

I shouted: "Dad, I'm coming to help you!"

The noise of digging stopped. After a while, Dad poked his head out of the opening, with crumbling dirt on his head.

Wearing a rather unhappy expression, he asked: "Why did you come here instead of going to class?"

"I want to dig the kiln with you!"

"I don't need your help." Dad was very angry.

I hurriedly told my dad my plan and promised him that it would not affect my studies. If he didn't let me help him, I would not be able to concentrate in lessons, and this would definitely affect my studies.

"Dad, believe me. I can balance my studies and firing charcoal with you."

The hard lines on Dad's face slowly relaxed. I knew he was in agreement.

The moment Dad came out of the opening of the kiln, I went inside. I wanted to see how much progress he had made. Inside, it was very dark and quite narrow as well. Clods of dirt that he had dug up were scattered on the ground. My stomach was growling. I got out of the kiln in a hurry.

"Dad, let's eat. I'm hungry!"

"You haven't had your lunch? Didn't you bring it to school this morning?"

"I have brought it here. Last time when I went to see Mum in the health centre, she said the food I brought to her was delicious. Dad, I want to eat with you too."

Dad smiled and said: "Well, let's eat together then."

He cut down a small bamboo and quickly made two pairs of chopsticks. We sat on the chopped wood and took turns to eat the food in my lunch mug.

After we finished, I asked: "Dad, is my lunch delicious?"

Dad said: "You bet!"

After lunch, we went to the river, bent down and put our mouths to the surface to drink our fill. That felt so good.

Dad said: "There's some porridge in the pot too. Let's work for a while, and then we can drink it. The inside of the kiln is still very small. If we both get inside, there'll be no space for us to turn around. So, I'll do the digging while you'll be in charge of moving the clods of earth with your hoe. We'll do the work together, and it'll get done faster."

When he finished, he entered the cave again, and the thwacks of digging resumed.

I picked up my long-handled hoe and got into the cave. When my eyes had adjusted to the light and I was sure that I wouldn't hurt my dad by accident, I tried my best to hook the earth out of the cave with my hoe. Within a short period of time, I was sweating all over. Following my dad, I took off my coat and long trousers, leaving only my shorts.

Dad said: "Lejiang, take a rest when you're feeling tired. Digging a charcoal kiln is hard work. It's not something that can be done overnight."

I said: "I'm not tired. I can carry away as many clods of earth as you can dig up."

I did my work vigorously, and I really didn't feel tired at all. I hooked the clods of earth to the entrance of the cave and then used my hoe to throw them away; they would roll down the slope and into the Bachi River. Those clods of earth stirred up the river, and many small fish swam over and played in the muddied water, thinking they might find something delicious. I was worried that the rolling clods of earth might hurt them.

Beside the thwacks of digging dirt, my dad's moo-like singing of *jiate* could be heard from time to time. When he sang the second and third times, I became familiar with it and began singing with him.

> *Liao luo wei,*
> *Holding a hoe in my hands,*
> *Dig a charcoal kiln that looks like a room;*
> *Not afraid of sweating*
> *For my son and my family.*

It was getting dark, so we headed home. Along the way, we talked about sharing the housework – who would do this and who would do that – so that we could finish everything soon after we arrived home. But when we got home, Dad and I were really surprised to see that Mum had already cooked the dinner, chopped plant leaves for the pigs and finished cooking our meal.

Dad scolded her out of concern. "You silly woman, you haven't completely recovered yet."

Mum said: "I know, and I'll be careful. I won't do any heavy work like feeding the pigs."

I said to her: "Mum, I helped Dad dig the charcoal kiln today."

"I guessed that – otherwise, you would have been home much earlier."

Dad said: "Lejiang is a very good assistant. His help really speeds up the digging work!"

Mum was very happy. "Really? Lejiang, come here."

She kissed me lovingly and said: "Lejiang, having a son like you is a blessing. I wish I could have ten sons like you."

Dad smiled and said: "Stop daydreaming! When we were allowed to have a second child, you said we should wait until life gets better. Years have passed, and now family planning policy is in force, so we can only have one. No more talk of having ten children."

He was right. Some ethnic minorities could have their own policies, but we Zhuang people had a large population and the family planning policy applied to us in the same way that it applied to the Han nationals. So my hopes of having a younger brother or a younger sister would never be fulfilled. It was the same for Lemin, Leping and Yisong. As a girl, Cuiyun could have one more brother or sister, but her dad died early and her mother remarried, so she was an only child too. That was probably why we five felt so close, like real sisters and brothers.

After finishing our homework in the evening, Lemin said that the afternoon lessons were music and physical education, so they offered to teach me the new song. But I suddenly felt very tired – so tired that no matter how hard I tried, I just couldn't keep my eyes open. I fell asleep over the table. I was totally unaware of when my friends left and how my dad took me to my bed. I was too tired.

26
HARD PHYSICAL LABOUR

On the way to school the next day, I asked my friends why they had left my home before teaching me the new song. They all laughed and said I had fallen into a deep sleep by that time, so how could they do it?

They began to teach me the song as we continued on our way to school. When we finally arrived, Yisong said: "Shall we pass Brother Jiang?"

As for physical education, they had been taught a new horizontal bar move. Our classmates had not arrived at school yet, so I ran to the playground, switched on the torch and began to learn the move. With my friends' help, I mastered it quickly.

Over the next few days, I insisted on going to help my dad and keeping up with my studies at the same time.

The charcoal kiln was getting bigger and bigger. On the day after we cleaned up all the earth we had dug up, Dad looked around the kiln shell, measured it with his hoe and said: "Now the kiln is big enough to make a thousand pounds of charcoal in one burning. It won't work if it's too small, and it will take too much time to make charcoal if it's too big. It looks perfect as it is now. Let's do the chimney work."

I asked: "How big should it be? Let me do this."

Dad asked me: "What's your plan?"

"Build one right down through the roof of the kiln."

Dad said: "If you were to build a chimney like this, the kiln would yield ashes or unburnt wood. The intake opening of a chimney should be lower than the ground. Let's improve the opening of the kiln again. It's better to keep the flame from burning the wood directly and let it rise along the kiln wall to the top. Only this way will the heat of the fire go down from the top of the kiln to dry the moisture in the wood. Then, the smoke and moisture will go out through the chimney built close to the ground, and all the wood inside the kiln can be carbonised evenly and turn into more charcoal. The quality of the charcoal will be particularly good too. But now I'm wondering how many chimneys we will need. Some people build one, and some prefer two or three. Our kiln is moderate in size so let's make two."

Looking at the top of the kiln, Dad said: "The arch is not high enough, so the flame will reach the wood too fast, which means the wood near the top of the kiln will be burnt to ashes."

We shovelled the top of the kiln to increase its height and dug a ditch about a foot wide and half a foot deep along the bottom of the kiln. Then, along the kiln wall, in a place where it formed the shape of the character *pin* against the opening of the kiln, we cut two deep grooves using a shovel with a pointed tip. These grooves extended upward and led to the outside of the kiln. Dad got two bricks, covered them with mud and carefully laid them on the grooves to make them the same level as the kiln wall. The two chimneys were done.

Dad said: "It requires patience to build chimneys. Bricks must be laid tight without leaving any gaps – otherwise, heat will escape and fail to descend to the ground. If this happens, there will be more half-burnt charcoal, which is usually regarded as dry firewood. The quality of the chimney is directly related to the quality of the charcoal."

It was indeed hard work. It took us two whole days to build the two chimneys. Alongside my dad, I did my work patiently, watching carefully and remembering everything in my heart. I thought there might be one day after I grew up when something urgent would happen and I might have to make charcoal too.

I told my dad what I was thinking. He said: "You probably won't need to do this. Our country is reforming and opening-up to the outside world, so life will keep getting better with the current development. I believe a life like ours right now won't exist anymore. If it had not been for my building a lychee orchard and cutting down a lot of wood, I wouldn't have thought of making charcoal."

But mastering a life skill wouldn't do me any harm, would it?

The charcoal kiln was finished, but the next task – piling wood inside the kiln – was also hard work. Dad waved his sharp axe to prune and cut the logs into several pieces and then carried them into the kiln. We let the wood stand upright against the kiln wall and piled it up tight, layer after layer, to the top of the kiln. The pieces were all hardwood, and most of them didn't have a thick trunk, so they were not too heavy for me to carry on my shoulder. We placed the pruned branches and leaves beside the opening of the kiln for burning.

Once all of the wood was piled inside the kiln, my dad's vision for a lychee orchard appeared clearly before us. It stood beside the river, facing south, and it was on fertile land. More importantly, the whole piece of land was at a high elevation, so even if the Bachi River became heavily flooded, it would not do harm to the orchard.

Full of admiration for my dad, I said: "Dad, you're so wise to choose this area for the lychee orchard!"

"It's been a long time since I had the idea to create a lychee orchard. My wish is to further your second great-uncle's work," said my dad.

With all the wood inside the kiln, my dad began to build a burner at the opening. He said: "There are two ways to make charcoal. One way is to burn the kiln with someone watching all the time. The other is to build a large burner, put in a few hundred pounds of dry wood, ignite it and leave it. The second way takes more time, and I'm not sure whether it will work, so we'd better watch it when it's burning. Hard as it will be, we'll get more charcoal of high quality."

Dad built a wall inside the kiln so that the fire would not burn the wood directly. Instead, it would rise up at an angle to the top of the kiln, giving heat to all the wood.

I asked Dad: "How long does it take to fire a kiln of charcoal?"

"I guess we need three firings. The humidity of each charcoal kiln is different, and the wood varies as well. The time to seal the kiln is determined by the smoke from the chimneys."

In our village, one firing lasted for twelve hours.

Dad decided to burn the kiln that night. He had already set up a shed with branches. After supper, he would carry his bedding there.

I said: "Dad, let me fire the kiln with you, please."

"No!" Dad said. There was no room for negotiation. "From now on, you must go to school like the other children. You can't stay with me tonight. Uncle Bofu has promised to help me. Go back to school and concentrate on your studies."

"When did I ever fail to concentrate on my studies?" I retorted. I felt wronged.

"Well, then concentrate more!"

I thought about it and said: "Dad, I have a request."

"What is it?"

"I want to see what the smoke from the chimneys looks like when you have sealed the kiln."

Dad looked pleased and said: "You want to know the whole process of making charcoal? You really think you might make charcoal in the future when you grow up? OK, I'll tell you when the time comes."

Dad and Uncle Bofu slept in the shed beside the kiln that night. I had planned to cook lunch by myself in the morning, but I couldn't manage to do it. Mum said I slept like a log – so soundly that I would not wake up even if someone should carry me and throw me into the Bachi River. It was Mum's sweet *liaoluo* that eventually stirred me, and it was she who limped and prepared breakfast and lunch.

I was ashamed and said: "Mum, I shouldn't let you do so many things for me."

Mum said: "I can move around. I'm so happy whenever I think about it."

In the afternoon after school, Mum said: "Lejiang, go and take some food to Dad and Uncle Bofu."

"Dad took a cooking pot with him, didn't he?"

"I killed a chicken and made a dish for them," Mum said. "Firing a kiln is hard work. We don't have the money to pay labourers to do this."

Mum had made a chicken dish that everyone loved, a large plate inside a bamboo basket. Next to the plate was half a bottle of homemade rice wine and a small bowl of dip made of green onion, finely minced ginger and soy sauce. As I opened the lid of the bamboo basket, the seductive scent of chicken attacked my nostrils, and the chicken's skin looked golden brown. My mouth watered.

"One chicken leg is for you. Go to the kiln and eat it with your dad. It's a small chicken that doesn't have much meat. I cut the other chicken leg into pieces for your dad and Uncle Bofu," said Mum.

"Mum, what about you?"

"I've eaten already."

I could see clearly that the whole chicken was on the plate and Mum hadn't had a piece of it.

"OK," I said. I turned around and secretly picked up three pieces of thick chicken breast, dipped them in the sauce and left them in a small bowl for Mum.

When I ran to the charcoal kiln, Uncle Bofu was adding firewood to the burner. The fire was burning brightly, and white smoke was billowing out of the two chimneys.

Dad was lying in the shed resting. When he heard me, he rubbed his eyes and sat up.

"Dad, Mum asked me to bring you chicken."

Dad opened the basket and cried happily: "Wow, steamed chicken! And rice wine!"

"Dad, you and Uncle Bofu should take your time enjoying the chicken. Let me watch the fire."

I grabbed the chicken leg, dipped it in the sauce and went to sit in front of the burner. I added wood to the burner as I ate the chicken leg.

Dad and Uncle Bofu sat on the ground in the shed and passed the wine bottle to each other, taking a drink in turns. They picked the chicken up with their fingers and ate heartily. Uncle Bofu exclaimed: "I truly admire your wife's cooking. Isn't steamed chicken made with boiling water? But her version tastes so different from others! Crispy skin and tender, flavourful meat!"

The fire was glowing in the burner, and flames dashed upwards to the top of the kiln making a loud whistling sound. Soon, I was sweating all over from the burning fire, and I realised what hard work firing a kiln could be. If there was another option, no one would choose to do such physical labour.

Dad told me, judging by the smoke coming from the chimney, that the charcoal kiln could be sealed after three firings. That meant they could seal the kiln the following morning. I would be sitting in the classroom listening to a lesson at that time, so I wouldn't be allowed to watch.

Dad explained: "Look at the smoke from the chimney. It's white, isn't it? That's the moisture. A small portion comes from the kiln wall, but most of it is the moisture squeezed out of the wood by the heat. When some blue smoke appears with the white, it means the wood close to the top of the kiln has no moisture left and has become charcoal. We call this stage *jiehuo*. The kiln will be sealed after we can see that all the wood has become charcoal."

"How do we seal the kiln?" I asked.

Dad said: "The first thing we have to do is block the two chimneys to stop air circulation inside the kiln. The second thing is to build another wall outside the opening of the kiln. Then, we pour a few dozen cups of water into the burner and leave it to cool down gradually. There's a fire wall inside the kiln that will block the water from the charcoal. The final step is to seal the opening of the kiln to stop the fresh air from getting inside. When all this is done, we can open the kiln and get the charcoal out five or six days later. By then, all these charcoal baskets will be full."

I looked around and saw that my dad had already filled many of the big charcoal baskets.

After hearing what he said, I felt I understood well in theory, but I still wasn't confident to do it. In fact, the most important thing was to make a judgement about whether the wood had already become charcoal according to the smoke coming from the chimney, that is, mastering the skill of timing. Without practice, there was no way to acquire this understanding.

Dad postponed the opening of the kiln to Saturday. For one thing, he wanted to make sure all the charcoal inside the kiln had cooled down. More importantly, the next day would be Sunday, and I could help him take the charcoal to Baodong. A helper was indispensable when sailing up the river to Baodong; to cross Laimu Sandbank, we had to pass through a waterway on its right bank where the navigation channel was narrow with rapids, and it was very hard to pass by sailing the boat single-handedly.

We made an early start on Saturday. Lemin, Leping and Yisong had long decided to help my dad get the charcoal out of the kiln, so we took a shortcut and rushed there.

Dad had been working alone for a long time, and he had already filled a few baskets. His face and body were dyed black as if painted by ink.

"Dad, take a rest. Let us try."

A heatwave hit me as I entered the kiln. It was extraordinarily hot inside – quite suffocating. I quickly grabbed two charcoal sticks, handed them to Leping behind me and said: "Pass them out."

We passed the charcoal sticks round by hand until they reached my dad, who immediately placed them, nice and tight, into the charcoal baskets. When I could not do it any more, Lemin would take my place. Like this, we four, taking turns, got the charcoal out of the kiln. We worked in high spirits, and glossy black charcoal sticks flew out of the kiln, on and on, and were neatly placed into the baskets.

When Dad asked us to stop for a while, we looked at each other and laughed hysterically. We had become completely blackened.

Of course, we jumped into the Bachi River to take a bath, but at this time it was a little cold in the river.

27
SAILING ACROSS TO SHORE

My favourite thing was to row the boat with my dad. I paddled slowly, and we splashed forward along the river while my dad hummed his *jiate*. I had a feeling that it was me who was carrying him this time. In the past, I was the one who sat on my dad's shoulders as he walked. I suddenly felt I had grown up. What's more, not only was my dad onboard but there was also the charcoal baskets, filling our boat up completely.

The night before, Dad weighed all the charcoal baskets and loaded them onto the boat. We set out before daybreak. Lemin, Leping and Yisong were probably still dreaming as I was paddling the boat over and setting off up the river.

That morning, the river was particularly calm. The sound of fish leaping for food could be heard clearly. Above our heads, a few cries came to our ears. Dad said it was night herons. This nocturnal bird had dark, grey feathers, and I once saw one sleep with its head on one side in the bamboo bushes along the riverside.

The boat was heavy. Though I tried hard to paddle forward, it still moved quite slowly, and this caused me some anxiety.

It was getting light. Along the riverside, thrushes burst out into song, and they were later joined by pheasants, partridges and turtledoves. Chirping loudly, two kingfishers flew over our boat and then disappeared into the poplar trees by the river. They seemed to be laughing at our slowness.

Dad stood up. "Let me row the boat. We need to hurry up to get to Baodong before the vehicles departing from Beihai for Nanning arrive there."

Dad's big hands were really powerful, and our boat dashed forward, though he didn't seem to be exerting himself much. Perching on a poplar tree, the two kingfishers were left behind; they quickly flew away but didn't dare to fly in front of our boat.

The first sandbank we crossed was called Laihe. In the Zhuang language, *he* means 'grass', and Laihe therefore means a lot of grass grew on both sides of the sandbank. The name was still used, even though little grass was left there; it had become a bamboo forest. Laihe Sandbank was rocky. Four or five streams of water flew over rocks that crossed the river surface. The one in the middle was a navigation channel that was wider than a boat.

Dad stopped the boat beside some rocks. He asked me to get off the boat and wade to the navigation channel. Standing on a rock and holding the gunnel, he pulled the boat round to the other side of the rocks and into the waterway. He kept the bow in line with the navigation channel and pushed harder, while I, on the other side of the boat, grabbed the gunnel and pulled. Our boat passed through the channel quickly and safely.

One by one, we crossed the sandbanks of Laipo, Lailan and Lailiang in the same way. The channel at Laitian was wider than our boat, and it was the easiest one to handle. We didn't even need to get out – our boat passed through it smoothly after Dad made a few forceful strokes and I, standing at the bow, pushed the bamboo pole into the water a few times to keep the direction.

By this time, the sun had already risen high, and we were getting hungry.

Dad stopped the boat in a shady place beside the river. He said: "After we cross the Laimu Sandbank, there isn't a long way to go to get to the Baodong Ferry. Let's fill our stomachs first."

I went to the cabin and took out a basket, inside which were some sweet potatoes Mum had cooked for us. I opened the basket, took out the biggest one and handed it to Dad. Then, I took another one for myself. Sitting at the stern, we peeled off the skins and ate them. They tasted especially sweet, like honey after being dried in the sun for a long time.

"Laimu Sandbank is the hardest one to conquer, so we need to gather our strength and take more care," said Dad.

Before we finished the thirty-*li* waterway, we encountered five more sandbanks that were similar to Laihe, Laipo, Lailan, Lailiang and Laitian. It wasn't surprising that no one in our village would take this waterway to Baodong unless they had heavy goods to carry. They preferred to walk the twenty-*li* mountain road to and from the market in Baodong.

Laimu was a rocky sandbank too, with the river running through the narrow passages between the rocks. All of the passages were narrow, so it was easy for a person to jump over the rocks to reach the other side of the river while boats couldn't. Unlike the other sandbanks, Laimu had a branch that ran along its south side like a winding mountain stream, having been washed out by the river. It was Laimu Sandbank's only navigation channel; all the boats would pass through there. Shaded by dense trees, the channel was wide enough to row a boat with two oars. It was not deep though, only reaching the waist of an adult. The fine yellowish sand on the riverbed could be seen clearly through the water. But this channel was known for its rapids, and it was particularly difficult to pass through with a boat.

Dad asked me to stand at the bow of the boat, holding the bamboo pole to control the direction while he paddled the boat hard.

As we were approaching the channel, I saw a long series of shadows struggling against the current under the water.

"Green bamboo carp are crossing the sandbank!" Dad said.

I now saw them clearly. A shoal of green bamboo carp, each weighing about five or six kilograms, were quickly moving their tails and rushing forward, none of them stopping for a second.

Dad began to sing:

> *Liao luo wei,*
> *How many turns has the Bachi River taken?*
> *How many shoals of green bamboo carps can swim across it?*
> *Why should we be afraid of heavy labour on the farmland?*
> *Good boys dare to swim against the current.*

This was Second Great-Uncle's *shan'ge*. I could sing it as well, and I joined in. Our singing startled a few water rails that were bending their heads to look for food along the riverside. Unable to fly far, they could only get into the bushes, crying noisily.

"Lejiang, cheer up and take care!" warned Dad, rowing at the stern.

"Don't worry Dad, I will." Standing on the bow, I pushed the bamboo pole into the river, right and left, to keep the boat moving in the right direction.

I thought that the boat was passing through quite smoothly, and it was not as difficult as my dad had warned me. Dad had stopped singing his *jiate*, but I continued:

> *How many turns has the Bachi River taken?*
> *How many shoals of green bamboo carps can swim*
> *across it?*

"Pay attention! We're turning now!" Dad shouted.

The bow turned to the right and entered a steeper rapid where the water rushed down towards the port side of the boat. I was not ready for this. I had tried my best to push the bamboo pole into the water on the left side of the bank so that our boat could make a turn and sail upstream, but I didn't have enough strength, and before I could pull the bamboo pole out of the water, the rapid pushed the boat and pressed the bamboo pole tight. I made every effort to pull it back but failed and had to let it go; if I had held on, I would have fallen into the water with it. Without the support of the bamboo pole, the bow of the boat hit the tree roots at the riverbank. The boat lost its balance, and the three charcoal baskets that were resting on the deck at the bow flopped into the river.

"Don't panic! Squat steady!" Dad shouted. He quickly let go of the paddles and jumped into the river. Standing in the rapids, Dad held the boat with one hand and stretched out his other hand to grab the charcoal baskets that were slowly sinking. He managed to put them back on the bow, one by one. I was panicking, and it took me quite a long time to recover. I jumped into the river to grab the bamboo pole and put it back on the boat. Then, I held on to the gunnel and helped Dad push the boat.

Dad said: "You three charcoal baskets are too naughty. Without a word, all of you jumped into the water. Did you want to wash your bodies white? Well, you failed! What's more, you have made yourselves cheap. Originally you could have been sold at six *jiao* per *jin,* but now you're worth only four *jiao* per *jin*. Don't you regret it?"

The charcoal didn't know what regret was, but I knew. I was so full of regret that my tears flowed.

My dad and I pushed the boat through the rapids of the navigation channel and stopped in a place with still water. We wrung out our wet clothes and set out again.

"Dad, it's all my fault! I didn't control the bow well."

"How could you be to blame? It's my fault," said Dad with a smile. "Lejiang, I overestimated your strength!"

When we arrived at Baodong Ferry, I found that the vehicles crossing it were all going from north to south, departing from Nanning and heading for Beihai. Nanning was much closer to Baodong than Beihai was. The Yongqin highway, a gravel road with many bends and slopes, was the only route from Nanning to Qinzhou and Beihai. When vehicles passed, they raised clouds of choking dust.

Dad said: "Those heading for Beihai rarely buy charcoal because people there sell it too. Our potential customers are heading for Nanning. But those heading for Nanning are ready to get onto the ferry the moment they arrive at the riverbank; they don't have the time to stop and buy charcoal. So we should move our charcoal to the north side of the river. When the vehicles get off the ferry, they'll have time to stop and buy charcoal."

We approached the pier at the north of the river. Before we reached our destination, a few sharp whistles came from the ferry where vehicles were getting on. One person pointed at us and shouted: "Move away quickly. You're getting in the way!"

"Dad!" I was trembling all over. Our boat was quite a few feet away from the ferry boat, so how could we be in its way?

Dad stopped rowing and said in a very humble tone to the man who was calling us: "Shifu, please allow us to carry the charcoals ashore first. There's no other place we can move the charcoal."

The man replied: "OK, do it quickly. Move your boat away at once when you've finished. If you don't, something bad might happen to you, and you'll regret it."

I had no idea what he was talking about. In our village, everyone spoke nicely and gently, and it was the first time I had heard someone be threatening like this. I didn't know where we had gone wrong; my face broke out into a nervous sweat, and I didn't know what to do.

Dad rowed the boat ashore and whispered to me: "Lejiang, don't be afraid. He was just talking in a loud voice. In fact, he was very kind. Get off the boat and hold it tight."

I quickly got off the boat and pulled the rope at the bow tightly. Dad carried all the charcoal baskets to the shore and said to the man on the ferry boat: "Shifu, let me row the boat away first. Then I'll be back to move the charcoal. I promise I won't inconvenience you."

The man didn't say anything but just waved his hands.

Dad docked the boat in a place far away from the pier. He then ran back and carried the charcoal baskets on his shoulder, one by one, to a spacious place on the roadside. He told me that vehicles had to speed up along the slope after they got off the ferry boat and it was not convenient for the drivers to stop to do business. We had to do more. I was not strong enough to carry a charcoal basket, so the only thing I could do to help my dad was carry the bamboo basket with sweet potatoes to the place where we would be selling.

Dad was right! Vehicles from Nanning didn't show any sign of stopping. They brought clouds of dust that blocked out the sun and then creaked while slowing down towards the pier. After they passed the river, they roared uphill with a few loud horns and then disappeared.

Dad and I stood behind our charcoal baskets and waved to all the passing vehicles patiently. But it didn't work at all. It was hard to burn charcoal, but it was not easy to sell it either. Every penny was hard to earn.

A grass-green Liberation lorry from Nanning stopped in front of us. The driver's window rolled down with a squeak, and a man poked his head out. He took off his sunglasses and asked kindly: "Selling charcoal?"

I sensed a glimmer of hope for the first time.

Dad answered hurriedly: "Yes, we're selling charcoal!"

"Is it good charcoal?"

"All good charcoal. Made of hardwood. Shifu, please come and have a look."

"I was just asking. I'm not buying. I'm in a hurry to deliver goods to Xiaodong Town."

The window closed with another squeak. The engine started noisily, and the lorry moved on to the ferry, leaving us choking dust. My hope died again.

Dad said: "It's normal that lorry drivers from Nanning don't buy charcoal. It stands to reason. Let's wait patiently for lorries from the south." I knew he was being self-depreciating, but what he was saying was true. We had to wait patiently under the scorching sun. Dad and I knew that only by selling all the charcoal could we get the money we urgently needed. If no one came to buy our charcoal, we would get nothing.

I wondered if one section of the highway from Baodong to Qinzhou and Beihai had collapsed. How could there not be a single lorry coming from the south for such a long time?

It felt like we had been waiting for ages by the time we finally saw a lorry being driven slowly onto the ferry at the opposite bank. The ferry boat carried it across, moving slower than a snail despite the fact that many people were pulling the rope hard.

When the lorry got off the boat, it drove on and approached us, snorting noisily like an old bull. Dad and I waved to it hopefully, but it simply ignored us and whistled by, faster than a rabbit.

I was extremely disappointed. Putting down my hand, I uttered a long sigh and said: "Well, it looks like lorries from Beihai don't want to buy charcoal either."

Dad said: "We can't expect all of the lorries to stop and buy charcoal. One in ten will be good enough."

The sun was already setting in the west. More than ten lorries from the south had passed by on their way north, one after another, but none of them stopped and asked about our charcoal.

"Lejiang, eat some sweet potatoes if you're hungry!" Dad was looking a bit helpless too, but he was more experienced than me and therefore had more patience.

"I'm not hungry," I said. In truth, I was hungry, but when I saw the baskets of charcoal left unsold, I had no appetite at all.

Just as I was about to give up hope, a lorry drove up from the ferry and stopped beside us. When the door of the truck opened, I recognised that the driver was the man who had told us he was delivering goods to Xiaodong Town. Xiaodong was much closer than Qinzhou or Beihai, and this man had returned after finishing his work.

"Haven't you sold your charcoal yet?" he asked as he jumped down from his cabin.

"Not yet. Shifu, these are all good. Please buy some," Dad said.

The man didn't answer. He took two charcoal sticks from the basket and tapped them together. They made a light metallic sound.

"Great charcoal!" the man said.

"All hardwood and fully burnt," Dad explained.

"Do they have long unburnt heads?" He raised one corner of a charcoal basket and carefully looked inside.

"We kept the fire moderate. The unburnt part was about five inches long," Dad said. "But we have already cut it off. We don't want people to burn charcoals that still give off smoke."

"You did?" He didn't seem to believe my dad's words. Dad once told me that many people who sold charcoal would mix unburnt parts with good charcoal. It seemed it was not the first time this man had bought charcoal.

I said: "Uncle, you can check the baskets yourself, one by one. Those that had unburnt parts all have cut marks left by the knife or axe."

He seemed to believe what I said and didn't check them. Instead, he rubbed his hands, turned to Dad and said: "I want to buy all of the charcoal. How much will you charge for that?"

"Sixty cents per *jin*."

"That's a bit expensive. Can you make it cheaper?"

"Shifu, how much do you want to pay?"

"Fifty cents per *jin*. What do you think?" The man glanced at the charcoal.

"Fifty cents?" Dad was hesitant, but when he saw that the man truly wanted to buy all of the charcoals, he finally agreed.

The man saw that three baskets had been put aside. "What happened to these?" he asked.

"Oh, there's a story behind that. When we crossed the sandbanks, these three baskets fell into the water. They're worth less after being soaked. If the other charcoals are sold at fifty cents per *jin*, I could at most charge thirty cents per *jin* for these three baskets."

My heart ached, and tears suddenly rolled down my face uncontrollably.

The man walked closer to the three baskets. "Oh? I can't even notice anything."

"Having been bathed under the sun for such a long time, the surface has dried. If you don't look carefully, you won't see it," Dad said.

The man turned his head and saw my tears. He said half-jokingly: "Boy, why do you cry? You can't bear to sell the charcoal to me?"

Dad didn't know what to say, so he just smiled.

I wiped my tears and said: "No, I'm just so sad. We borrowed a lot of money for my mum's medical treatment, but because of my carelessness, these three baskets fell into the river."

"Oh, I see." His smile faded, and he asked my dad about my mum's situation. "How much charcoal do you have in total? I want it all."

Dad said: "I've already weighed these. The net weight of each basket is fifty *jin* – ten baskets of good charcoal equals five hundred *jin*, and three baskets of wet charcoal equals one hundred and fifty *jin*. Let's weigh it again so that everyone will feel assured."

The man said: "There's no need. If I don't believe you, will there be anyone I can trust?"

Dad said: "What if I read the scales wrong?"

"I'm one hundred percent assured by what you said. You wouldn't have got it wrong. Let's load the charcoal onto my lorry."

Dad wanted to load the charcoal baskets onto the lorry, but the man wouldn't let him do it on his own. Together, they carried the baskets, each holding one side, and put them onto the lorry. Then, the man got into the driver's cabin, came back with a wad of money and said to Dad: "Forget the price I just mentioned. Let's do it according to the price you quoted originally."

He counted out a stack of banknotes and put them in my dad's hand. They were all ten-yuan notes, known as *datuanjie*, with images of workers, peasants, soldiers and the representatives of all ethnic groups on one side and the grand Tiananmen on the back. The man said: "Four hundred yuan in total. Put it away."

Dad was deeply moved and said: "That's too much – I can't accept it. But if you insist, those three baskets of wet charcoal are free."

The five hundred *jin* of good charcoal was worth just three hundred yuan. I said to the man hurriedly: "Uncle, you have given us one hundred yuan too much."

He had already returned to the driver's cabin and restarted the engine. He poked his head out of the window and said: "It's nothing. Keep that few yuan. It's a little something from me."

Dad quickly peeled off ten ten-yuan notes to return to the driver, but it was too late. In the blink of an eye, the lorry was gone.

Dad muttered: "Lejiang, we have met a man with a heart of gold."

"Dad, I have memorised that man's face and the licence plate number. I'll look for a chance to repay his kindness in the future."

Patting me on the shoulder, Dad said: "Yes, we should do that. Lejiang, you have grown up!"

28

HAPPY WINTER HOLIDAY

In order to help my dad transport charcoal to Baodong for a second time, I had to take a Monday off school. I asked Lemin to submit the absence note to Teacher Ma and told my friends to listen attentively in class so that they could help me make up for it later. While their torches shone on the mountain road leading to our school, mine was taking me and my dad to the charcoal kiln.

With our previous experience, we didn't make any mistakes, and the charcoal rested safely on the boat all the way. Unlike the previous day, everything went well when we sold the charcoal, and we no longer felt anxious. Many drivers stopped to buy from us. They didn't buy a lot – usually two baskets per person, and most of them paid six *jiao* per *jin* without haggling. The charcoal was gradually disappearing, and very soon all of it moved from country folk with a rural *hukou* to city dwellers with an urban *hukou*. This time, we had thirteen baskets of charcoal, and these netted us a total of three hundred and ninety yuan – thirty-nine ten-yuan banknotes. It was indeed a handsome income.

Dad was very happy. We decided not to eat the cooked sweet potatoes left in the basket. We went to a street in Baodong and had a bowl of freshly made rice noodles with basil.

Time flew. The final exam was around the corner, and we had been walking to school on the ten-*li* mountain road for a term. Though I had experienced so many things, I didn't fall behind my classmates. Hand in hand, we four worked hard and ranked in the top ten of our class. Leming, Leping and Yisong also won the Triple Honour Student award which recognised good academic performance, good health and good morals. I didn't get it because I had taken so many days off, but I was not sad – I was pleased for my friends.

We embraced the winter holidays in a happy mood. On our way back to the village, we rushed to Genma Ridge and had a discussion about how we would spend our time off school.

"I want to play to my heart's content!" Yisong said. "Blacky likes to have fun – he always wants me to take him to the mountain."

"I'm afraid you won't have much time to play," Leping said. "Yesterday, my dad told me that we'll start sawing wood as soon as the winter holiday begins."

Lemin jumped up. "Oh, I almost forgot about the watermill."

I had forgotten about it too. Perhaps adults didn't want to let it distract us from our studies. My dad hadn't mentioned it again. I said to my friends: "Sawing is hard work, but no matter how busy and tired we should be, we must keep on learning. At night, we should study together as usual, concentrating on our winter holiday assignments."

My friends all agreed.

When we reached The Immortal Watching the Moon, I suddenly thought of something and said to them: "Let's go to the navel to take a look."

"You mean to visit the mother fox?" asked Yisong.

"She won't be back there," said Lemin.

I said: "Let's go to check the bullet trees there and see whether bullets are growing well."

"Yes, I noticed that the bullet trees there bear a lot of fruit. They were still small when I saw them last time."

We ran there and shouted together happily. Great! Bunches of fruit, a bit larger than soya beans, hung on the tree and bent the branches down. It was the perfect time for picking bullets. These wild fruits would ripen quickly and become soft and black. The birds loved to eat them, but we didn't. Now that they were half ripe, uniform in size, especially round and moderately soft, they made the perfect bullets for toy guns. That's why we called them bullet trees. They were a kind of hardwood, and nobody knew their real name. The adults liked to chop them down for firewood because they were hard and they burnt easily, so it was very difficult to find good bullets around our village at that time.

We rushed down there, and each of us picked up a large handful of bullets.

"I'm sure my gun will win the first prize this time," said Leping.

I advised: "Your gun is good, but it gets stuck easily because the passage from the magazine to the barrel is too large. You might think that the bullets would move more smoothly through a larger space, but the opposite is true – the larger the passage, the more likely it is that they will crowd together and fail to reach the barrel."

"Oh, I see. No wonder it gets stuck!" said Leping. "I was confused about this. Your explanation is very helpful, Brother Jiang."

Yisong had no confidence at all. "I don't think I can compete with you guys. I might as well just bring Blacky to the mountain."

Once I got home, I put down my school bag and ran out to look for the right bamboo to make a gun barrel. Bamboo used for weaving materials wouldn't have been suitable because the inner diameter would be too large and could only be used to make a magazine. I found a shoulder-pole bamboo with the correct inner diameter, cut it into a few pieces and made a pistol overnight.

In winter, playing with toy guns was our favourite pastime. At first, we played single shot. It was pretty easy. You placed the gun barrel in position, fixed the trigger, pushed the first bullet close to the muzzle, and then did the second one quickly. The compressed air would expel the first bullet while the second bullet stopped naturally at the muzzle. Shots would go like this one by one. We had strict rules for this game. We would be scored on sound, range and accuracy. Shooting at a person was strictly forbidden. Though the bullets were merely tiny wild fruit, they truly hurt when they hit the body, and there was also the danger that they could damage your eyes. What's more, they contained juice that would stain your clothes.

As we got older, we stopped playing single shot and moved on to 'machine gun', which involved firing in rapid succession.

I dug a barrel with a knife, put on the magazine and made a trigger with the hardest *ganle* bamboo. Mum found me a weaving bobbin, and I installed it on the trigger as a handle so that it would be easier for me to hold the gun. Finally, I twisted a fine hemp rope to fasten the trigger in the right position on the barrel. This way, the trigger would stay in place even if I pushed and pulled it with my eyes closed. I placed a handful of bullets into the magazine to test the gun. *Bratat bratat bratat.* The gunshots were loud and continuous.

After some careful planning, I made a machine gun too. It was more beautiful than the first one.

At the break of dawn, we gathered at the Wangpa Ferry with the adults. The winter holidays had started, and we had to saw the wood as planned.

Yisong was the first to arrive. He was with Blacky, who was squatting in front of me as if pleading for his master. Yisong said: "Brother Jiang, do me a favour – tell me what's wrong with my gun?"

I took the gun and tried it. The bullet could not be fired; instead, it just fell out of the muzzle. "The barrel is too big. Air leaks at both ends, so it won't fire loudly."

"What should I do?" asked Yisong anxiously.

"Put it aside until you find the right bullets." I handed him the extra gun I had made and said: "Try this."

Yisong fired the gun, and sharp sounds burst out. His sadness gave way to laughter.

When the adults discovered we were going to have a shooting competition, they rowed their boats and lined them up in the river. I shouted: "Three, two, one, fire!" The four guns fired at the same time, creating a sharp *bratat* sound on the surface of the river. The bullets flew a long way and finally fell into the water, like raindrops.

At this crucial moment, Leping's gun broke with a crack. He had pushed the trigger too hard. His gun was completely finished, so that was the end of his shooting. His face went bright red.

Four adults served as our judges. Yisong was awarded first place because his gun sounded the loudest and it had the longest range.

Yisong could not tear himself away from that gun. "Brother Jiang lent me this. It's great," he said.

"Did Brother Jiang lend you the best gun?" asked Leping enviously.

Uncle Boping said: "Lejiang is a real man. When lending something to his friends, he is sure to choose the best."

We continued to play as we rowed the boats along the river, and very soon we arrived at Jinzhang. A lot of tall pine trees grew there, and it was a place where the cutting down of trees for personal use was allowed. As long as the village committee approved, anyone could go to select and cut down trees in this place. In our language, *jin* means 'deep valley'. It's likely that musk deer lived there in the past, so it was given the name 'Jinzhang'. Walking into the valley, we saw the place that the adults had designated for sawing wood. A few large pine trees had already been chopped down and cut into pieces about six feet long. Ink lines were drawn on the logs, which were then shaped into squares with axes. Four square logs were lined in a row along the slope, each of them resting in a dirt pit with their cutting edges up in the air. Large saws were hanging down from them, waiting for us to begin our work.

Standing on one of the square logs, Dad said: "You four, come and watch how to saw this." He held the saw handle while Uncle Boping stood under the log holding the other handle. When Dad pulled the saw, Uncle Boping would help push it upward. It made a loud whirring sound. Uncle Boping then pulled it downward, and Dad pushed it down at the same time. The saw's teeth bit into the wood, and the sawdust fell off like snow.

As he was sawing, Dad explained: "When the saw moves upward, the one who stands below should first lift it up gently and then push, not letting the teeth bite into the wood. Otherwise, the saw will meet with more resistance which requires much more effort. When pulling it downwards, exert a little more pressure, but don't go to extremes. This work won't be completed with only a few pulls and pushes – it takes a few days." Dad stopped the saw and said: "Align the saw with the ink line, or it will cut a wavy shape and spoil the wood."

Dad and Uncle Boping demonstrated a few more times before Dad said: "You're still young and can only stand under the log. Well, who wants to try first?"

"Me first!" Leping stood in his dad's position, spat on his palms and held the handle of the saw. The sound of whirring burst out.

Dad said: "Great job! Next!"

When it was Yisong's turn, I asked Leping in a whisper: "Is it difficult?"

"Not at all."

I was the last one to try the saw and felt it was indeed not difficult. We all thought we could do it easily.

Standing in our respective positions, we each worked with our father. The sound of sawing rose and fell continuously. I thought that if there were musk deer in the valley, they must have been scared away by the noise we were making.

The work was new and exciting for us. Most people hated sawing wood, but we never felt that way about it. When the adults sang their *jiate*, we would join in with songs we had just learned at school. We didn't want to stop singing until the adults called out to announce that it was time for a break.

"We've finished one end, so it's time to do the other end. We need to sharpen our saws first because they've already been blunted. What's more, we must cook some porridge now," Dad said.

The adults fetched the spring water to cook the porridge. Then, they worked together to turn the square log around, preparing for the sawing of the other end. While they started to sharpen the saws' teeth with files, our task was to build a sweet potato kiln. We dug some mud and made a kiln in the form of an arch. Then, we set a fire inside the kiln, burning it red and hot. At the appropriate time, we extinguished the fire, spread the wood ash and threw some raw sweet potatoes into the kiln. The last step was to smash the kiln, break the red hot chunk of mud and spread it evenly on the sweet potatoes. Leaving it like this, we continued to do our sawing work.

Accompanying the continuous whirring sound of the saws, planks three inches thick and six inches long fell down, one by one.

The porridge was ready, and the sweet potatoes were cooked. We scratched away the mud, and the sweet potatoes beneath had burnt skins and gave off a tempting aroma.

After lunch, we continued our work, but I felt my hands were heavy, my arms were sore, and it was getting more and more difficult to push the saw upwards. When I looked up, I was shocked into silence. Why hadn't the saw aligned with the ink line? Why hadn't it cut straight along the line? Without daring to make a sound, I tried to bring the saw back to its correct position, which was not easy at all.

Dad said: "Bosong, come and help. We have a problem here."

I was surprised. "Dad, how did you know this?"

"I'm doing the sawing work, so how couldn't I know this?" Dad said.

Uncle Bosong came over. Yisong took the chance to plonk himself down on the sawdust. He seemed to be as exhausted as I was.

Uncle Bosong took the saw from my hand and moved it back a little. Then, he and Dad cut the wood along the ink line. The saw was now in its correct position.

"Let them take a rest when they have finished this log. They can only handle so much today," Dad said. After leaving our sawing positions, we all immediately sprawled on the ground.

The adults reorganised into two teams, Uncle Bosong paired with Dad, while Uncle Bomin paired with Uncle Boping. Two saws were raised high, and the whirring sound was particularly loud and long as they cut into the logs fast and deep.

When we studied together that evening under the bamboo-shoot lamp, we all slumped over the table and fell asleep. It was the first time this had ever happened. When I woke up the next day, I felt like my bones were coming apart, and I ached all over whenever I moved.

"You don't need to join us today. Take a day off," Dad said to me.

To be honest, I had thought about having a day off, but when I heard Dad say this, I blurted out without thinking: "No, Dad, I can't fish for three days while drying the nets for only two days!"

Dad burst out laughing and said: "You're right. And what's more, we've only fished for one day!"

Over the next few days, my arms became as numb as the logs, and I found it difficult to move at all, but none of us would give up halfway. Eventually, we became accustomed to this hard work; we no longer felt so tired, our muscles and bones were not hurting anymore, and the movement of the pulling and pushing of the saws in our hands became faster and smoother. Of course, we still insisted on studying together under the lamp every night; we had to review our books every day in order to retain their contents and make them a part of us.

When all the planks were ready, we put them into the boat and carried them to Laili Sandbank. The adults in our village had already replaced the dam-supporting frames with new pinewood and piled stones there. Large pine beams were loaded between the frames. After all the planks were shipped there, we inserted one end of a plank into the stone trough cut by our ancestors and nailed it tightly onto the big beam. After a few days' hard work, a dam made of pine stood up at Laili Sandbank in readiness for the spring floods. Though it looked flimsy, it was actually very strong. When the water rose, it rushed over the dam; soon after this, the water level above and below the dam would be equalised, allowing the water and floating debris to flow past. The wooden dam simply stood erect, and the wet pine would not rot for centuries. I was amazed that my ancestors had the wisdom to work out such a way to stop the river. They were so clever!

Leping wanted to have another shooting contest, and he had secretly made a new trigger. But all the bullet fruits were fully ripe now; many had been eaten by wild birds, while most of them had fallen to the ground. Without bullets, even the best guns became useless. The shooting contest had to be postponed until the next winter.

Another compensation of the sawing work during the winter holidays was that our arms became a lot stronger. The new term began soon after the Spring Festival, and when we had arm-wrestling contests, we four found no rivals in our class. Our classmates were greatly shocked.

Who was the victor among us four?

Leping, of course. But I cleverly let him win. I didn't tell anyone.

29

FOOTSTEPS OF SPRING

The rebuilding of our watermill was completed less than a month after the new term began. When the sluice gate was open, the waterwheel below the mill would rotate; this, in turn, made the two large stone wheels inside the mill roll slowly, making a pleasant murmuring sound and grinding the millet in the disc. My grandfather was the happiest. He said the grinding sound would cure his rheumatism. After the watermill began working, he was there almost all the time. The villagers no longer had to ship grain to Baodong for machine grinding; what's more, our watermill usually ground the rice intact, and the rice bran was very fine. Not only people in our village but also people from along the river loved to ship their grain here, so the sluice gate remained constantly open from day one.

Chasing the murmuring sound of the watermill, a cosy spring wind came. Mulberry trees at the edge of our village and beside the fields had grown dense young leaves overnight, like magic. Mum's leg injury had also completely recovered with the arrival of spring, which was indeed the happiest thing of all for me and my dad. Dad sang his *jiate* more often, which to my ears no longer sounded like the moo of bulls.

One morning, before I was leaving for school, Dad said: "The carp in the refuge pond of Forty have laid eggs. We've already put a few loads of water grass into the pool, and this has probably been fully covered with carp eggs.

If so, we can bring the eggs to live in the *wu*, and we won't need to worry about raising fingerlings in Forty this coming autumn."

I was overjoyed at hearing this, but I had a question. "Dad, wouldn't it be better for us to put the carp themselves into the *wu*? Then we could harvest all the eggs they will lay."

Dad said: "The water in the *wu* is quite different from river water. Carp feel more comfortable to lay eggs – more and better eggs – in the refuge pond than in the *wu*."

"Then why should we move eggs from the refuge pond to the *wu*? Wouldn't it be better for the eggs to be hatched in the refuge pond?"

"The *wu* is deep and quiet. Without natural enemies inside, it's more suitable for the small fry to grow. In the refuge pond, however, catfish and speckled fish are not vegetarians – they can eat a lot of small fry, so we'll only get very few in the end."

I was the kind of boy who loved to get to the bottom of things. "Since there are so many large carp in the Bachi River, wouldn't it be easier to put the water grass into the river and get the eggs there?"

Dad said: "It's a good idea, and I tried it once. It's true that there's a lot of large carp in the river, but there are also grass carp and green bamboo carp, and they feed on grass. The water grass we put into the river was almost gone within a day."

After school, we ran directly to Forty, full of curiosity. The refuge pond, under the slanting sun, was extraordinarily quiet as if nothing had happened, and it looked like there were no carp there. I walked into the water and picked up some water grass. I was amazed – it was covered with golden eggs. It was also the first time my friends had seen this; we were both surprised and joyful. I was afraid they would not hatch if they were out of the water for too long, so I hurriedly, but cautiously, put them back into the pond.

The adults arrived with dung baskets on their shoulders. We picked up four loads of water grass full of eggs, carried them back to the village and placed them into the *wu*. As I put the water grass into the water, I couldn't help saying: "This is your new home! Hatch and grow quickly. When the autumn comes, we'll pick you up, and you'll go back to Forty, your home."

Lemin said: "Brother Jiang sounds more like a poet when the spring comes."

The adults went back home while we stayed at the *wu*, full of hope, thinking about the day when small fry would emerge from the eggs.

Just at that time, a swarm of bees buzzed over our heads like a dark cloud. The spring was coming, and they were moving to their new home after separating from the old group.

"Hurry up!" I said to my friends before bending down, scooping a handful of sand and spreading it towards the bees. My friends realised what I had meant, and they did it too. The sand affected the flight of the bee colony, and it also blurred the eyes of the queen bee. They landed quickly and gathered in a ball under a fig tree. That was the way we had learned from adults to adopt a hive of wild bees.

Leaving my friends to watch over the bees in case they should fly away, I ran back home to get an old paddy basket and a sewing needle from my mum.

The queen bee was in charge of her family. I caught her and carefully tore her wings with the needle tip so that she could not lead her colony in flight again.

I put the queen bee into the paddy basket and then scooped the other bees in, one after another. Quickly, a beehive gathered around the queen. We brought it home, added a cover, opened a few small holes for the bees to go through and placed the hive in a sheltered place.

"It's a lucky day for us – the spring has sent us a bee colony," said Lemin.

"When we want to eat honey, we won't need to venture to Tunmeizhang anymore." Leping was, of course, very happy.

Mum seemed to be a different person. She worked more diligently and more tirelessly. She said: "I've been resting for a few months. Now, it's time for me to unleash all my strength!"

With Dad, she was busy working in the field, planting lychee trees, soaking grain seeds and spreading young seedlings. She also picked up fingerlings and put them into Forty. She was very busy from morning until night. Of course, she would still sing *liaoluo* to wake me up before dawn every day, and her voice was clearer and sweeter than ever.

Cuckoos, golden orioles and kingfishers with large heads all flew from the distant south. "Equinox, equinox, flutter the seedlings." This farming proverb told us it was time for us to transplant rice seedlings. We had a week's holiday for the busy farming season, so we were all dismissed from school and went back home to try our best to help with the family work.

On the first day of our holiday, we went to Forty very early in the morning. Dad, Uncle Bomin, Uncle Boping and Uncle Bosong had got there long ago to plough the field with four water buffaloes and four rakes. Mum and her three friends were not there; they went to Tunmeizhang to fetch the seedlings which had grown tall and strong.

Dad and his friends had already ploughed the field the day before, and the water in the field had been released. They had then built a mud dam between the refuge pond and the paddy field so that the muddy water in the field would not flow into the pool where the big carps that lay eggs lived.

When the adults ploughed the field, they stood in a row and moved forward, hand in hand. Driving the buffaloes, their shouts rang above Forty: "Right! Left! Move!"

My friends and I held our nets. Attached to each of our waists was a basin that floated on the water. Our task was to catch the first batch of carp we had raised inside Forty Paddy Field, and we fixed our eyes upon the surface. Four boats were lined up beside the river, near the paddy field. Their storage had already been unplugged, the water hole waiting for the fish to come in. For a long time, we didn't see any fish at all. I doubted they had all swum away, but a lot of wild arrowhead plants, as large as lychees, were floating on the surface. Fried arrowheads were tender and delicious – our favourite snack. During the planting season, our parents often picked them, and our pockets would be bulging. Since there were no fish to be seen, we began ladling arrowheads with our nets.

"Hey! You boys! Why aren't you catching fish?" Dad asked us loudly.

"Where are the fish then?"

"Follow them and keep your eyes tight on them!" Uncle Bomin shouted.

It turned out that after the adults had ploughed the paddy field, the water had become quite muddy and the fish had started to poke their heads out of the water for air. This was easy to miss if you weren't paying enough attention. We hurriedly poured the arrowheads onto the ridge of the field and waded to the adults, trying to catch a fish whenever we saw a mouth poking out of the water. Those mouths looked tiny, but they belonged to carp that weighed more than half a *catty* and were alive and kicking. These would now be called field carp, and they would be sold in Baodong. To keep them alive, we half-filled our basins with water, and when they were full of fish, we ran to the boat and put the fish into the storage.

It was such fun to catch carp in the paddy field. Shouting and chasing, we didn't have a care in the world. If one of us fell down and got covered with mud, everyone would break into happy laughter. There were so many fish in the paddy field, and soon all the storage areas were full.

Dad said: "Put them into the bamboo cages."

"Where are the bamboo cages?"

"Inside the refuge pond!"

The adults had made five large bamboo cages in advance. When they finished ploughing Forty Paddy Field, these cages were full of field carp weighing about half a *catty* each.

At this time, our mothers arrived with rice seedlings and cold porridge. We sat in a circle under the pine tree beside the field, drinking porridge with black olives as a side dish. How delicious the porridge was! No other delicacies could compete with it!

Mum lifted one bamboo cage inside the pool. The fish inside the cage were alarmed and thrashed about, splashing water on her face.

"So many of them! If we had known, we could have fried some to go with your porridge!" Mum said.

"Save that for supper. It's more important to beat the clock during the planting season," Dad said.

We did beat the clock. After eating lunch, we immediately transplanted the rice seedlings. Although Forty had been divided into four parts, no one family wanted to work alone because the grain and the seedlings were all the same. Four families decided to work together, finishing one family's share and then moving on to the next one.

Transplanting the rice seedlings was not as easy as catching the fish. Lined up in a row, twelve of us did the planting, working backwards. Our mothers were really fast. Their movements looked like chickens pecking grain on the ground, and our fathers were no match for them. Our mothers asked us to do the work beside them so that they could reach out their hands to help us transplant a few lines from time to time; they wanted us to follow what they were doing, but we were very clumsy and slow.

It didn't take long until we were aching all over and found it difficult to stand up straight, but we bit our lips and kept up with the adults. Swallows shuttled over the paddy field, and they sometimes flew low past us, chattering as if to praise our hard work.

After finishing the work in the field, our fathers did not stop to take a break but instead set off for Baodong in the middle of the night. Their boats, filled with fish inside the storage and towing large bamboo cages also filled with fish, were so heavy that they became increasingly difficult to row, and their speed slackened. The next day was market day in Baodong, so they had to set out in advance to arrive there on time.

The meat supply in the Baodong market was still inadequate. Our fresh and delicious field carp of moderate size was very popular and sold well. For all of us, that was the first income since the introduction of Land Distribution to Households. It made our fathers' *jiate* and our mothers' *liaoluo* more loud and enthusiastic.

Soon after the seedlings had been transplanted, silkworms started to emerge from their cocoons. Mum fed them tender mulberry leaves that had been dried and cut into pieces. They grew very fast, sleeping for seven days and shedding their skins for the first time. After they had shed their skins four times, they would climb onto the silkworm frames, spitting out silk and forming cocoons. At that time, the whole village formed a happy ensemble as the cocoons were reeled into raw silk.

When the farming season holiday was over, the adults asked us to take two buckets of field carp to school for our teachers. Our principal accepted the fish on behalf of the teachers, and they all said they were delicious. Our teachers later bought us a lot of extra-curricular books, which cost much more than those field carp.

After that, my friends and I would take a shortcut and run straight to our Forty Paddy Field after school, staring at the flourishing seedlings growing day by day and dreaming of the coming harvest.

As I sat on the edge of the field, my heart flew far away. Ah! The lofty Leimao Mountain, the rushing Bachi River, the thriving Forty Paddy Field! No matter where we go in the future, you will forever be in our memories and our hearts.

ABOUT THE AUTHOR

Huang Zheng, from China's Zhuang ethnic minority, is a member of the China Writers Association and the fourth, fifth and sixth director and editor of the Guangxi Writers Association.

He is a prolific author who is best known for his children's stories; these include the fantasy novel *Zhong Kui the Ghost Hunter*, the novella *The River and the Ridge*, and the short stories *The Honey Bee, Little Sister, Heart, In the Paddy Fields, Future Musician, Tian Xing's Great Escape, Lei Guo and Yong Ga*, and *Complementary Ideals*.

In 2019, *The River and the Ridge* was runner-up at the 2nd China National Ethnic Literature Prize hosted by the China Ethnic Literature Society. His children's radio drama *The Mother Looking for the Sun* won the Guangxi government's Bronze Drum Award. *Heart* won the first Guangxi Children's Literature Award.